AROMABINGO

DAVID GAFFNEY was born in V._
Birmingham and now lives in Manchester. He has worked as an
English teacher, a film studies lecturer, a holiday camp
entertainer, a medical records clerk, a pub pianist, a debt
counsellor in Moss Side, a legal consultant in Liverpool, and
now works for a shadowy government organisation. His stories
have been published in many magazines over the years and he
has made frequent appearances on the radio and at festivals.
David Gaffney's first collection, *Sawn-off Tales*, was published by
Salt in 2006 to critical acclaim.

Also by David Gaffney

Sawn-off Tales (Salt 2006)

DAVID
GAFFNEY
AROMA
BINGO

SALT

LONDON

PUBLISHED BY SALT PUBLISHING
Fourth Floor, 2 Tavistock Place, Bloomsbury, London WC1H 9RA United Kingdom

© David Gaffney, 2007, 2009

The right of David Gaffney to be identified as the
author of this work has been asserted by him in accordance
with Section 77 of the Copyright, Designs and Patents Act 1988.

First published 2007
This edition 2009

Printed and bound in the United Kingdom by Lightning Source UK Ltd
Typeset in Swift 10 / 12

ISBN 978 1 84471 342 4 hardback
ISBN 978 1 84471 546 6 paperback

1 3 5 7 9 8 6 4 2

For Susan, Sarah, Hannah, Kath and Tom.

CONTENTS

ACKNOWLEDGEMENTS

The author would like to extend his thanks to *Ambit* and *Modart* magazines in which where several stories from this collection have appeared, to *Flax* for publishing 'You and You Alone' and 'The Kids from Film Noir', to *Transmission* for 'Last Chance to Turn Around', 'The 1976 Trouser Famine' and 'The Half Life of Songs', to *Illustrated Ape* for 'Die Like a Rock', to *Cent Magazine* for 'Speaking in Pantone', to *Parameter* for 'The Happiness Well', to *The Quiet Feath*er for 'Great Inventions', to BBC Radio 3's *The Verb* for commissioning 'The Kids from Film Noir', 'You've Chosen to be Excited' and 'Are we Romping Now', to the-phone-book Limited for commissioning 'Guided by Voices' for The Burgess Project, *Citizen 32* for publishing 'Who Reads This Story Will Not Sin', and to East of the Web for publishing 'Gossammer' and 'This is about Dixie'. Thanks to *Lamport Court* for publishing 'The Secret Picture of David Cameron', to Manchester University and *Urbis* for selecting 'The Last Northerner' for the Manchester Monologue project.

PART ONE

45
REVOLUTIONS
PER MINUTE

ART MOVEMENT

HOWARD HAD NO talent for painting. He joined the class to meet attractive women and had a vague idea that if he developed a few basic skills they would pose naked for him. For this reason he had set up his easel next to Yvonne. Yvonne had remarkable hair—a neat black bob with the sheen of sump oil, and an unusual solidity, like a plastic hat. She also had an attractive way of nipping her lower lip between her teeth while she concentrated on her painting, which was a picture of a bird standing on an apple. Howard was about to mention that a bird probably wouldn't stand on an apple as the apple would roll away, when she leaned over and asked him, in a low whisper, if he had noticed that every colour of paint had its own little name written on the tube. Her voice was pleasantly croaky, as if she smoked a lot, and her bob of black hair brushed Howard's cheek as she spoke.

'Yes,' he whispered, with one eye on the tutor who could be rather strict about chatter. 'The yellow's called Buttercup Meadow.'

'Have you seen the name of the colour black? It is positively offensive,'

She thrust the tube into his face. Written on it were the words THE SILENCE OF DEATH.

He laughed. 'Creepy.'

3

'It's just not acceptable,' she said. 'For many, many, many reasons.'

Howard didn't know what she meant, but he liked the way her bob of black hair brushed his face and, because this sensation had suddenly become very important to him, he decided to agree with everything she said.

'Absolutely.'

'Why would death be silent?' Yvonne continued. 'When we meet up with our loved ones in heaven it will most certainly *not* be silent. It will be riotous! Chatting, singing, dancing. For example, my grandmother died last year and she hated silence—telly on full blast all day long.' She turned to her canvas and angrily squeezed out a curl of the offending colour. 'And another thing.' She swivelled violently, making her solid bob of hair swing. 'Why reserve this particular name for the colour black? If anything, death should be a colour that celebrates, it should be,' she clawed at the air for words, 'gold. The celebration of a new beginning. You know what this paint tube says to me?' She tossed it across the room, where it bounced off an easel and landed on the floor, spinning for a few seconds on the polished wood. 'It says that when you are dead there's nothing, and that is offensive to Jesus, and if it offends Jesus it offends me.'

∿

Howard and Yvonne entered the classroom by forcing a window with a screwdriver and used a torch to find their way about.

Squeezing all the black paint into one bowl and the gold into another was easy, but it was another matter entirely to put the black paint into the gold paint tubes and the gold paint into the black tubes.

4

'I'm getting it everywhere,' Yvonne said. 'I need to take my shirt off.'

'Me too.'

They stood there for a time, Yvonne in her bra, Howard's pale hairless chest shining in the amber light from the street lamp outside. Then he dipped his hand into the bowl of black and daubed a thick streak across her tummy. 'For Jesus,' he said.

'Keep going,' said Yvonne, and he did.

By the end of the night Howard's hands were caked and everything was gold and black. Yvonne was smothered in it. Even her immaculately clipped bobbed hair was clumped up in gluey golden peaks. The only parts of her that weren't gold and black were the palms of her hands where they'd been held together in prayer.

THE KIDS FROM
FILM NOIR

MY MOTHER AND father had been married for years before they discovered they'd both had full face transplants. What a hilarious coincidence. The problem was, because neither had seen the other's birth-face my poor mum and dad had no clue as to what any of their offspring might look like.

That's why at aged ten, when I looked in the mirror, Edward G. Robinson squinted back. The clinic had handed my parents the standard movie star catalogue to choose a gene cocktail, and they'd gone straight for film noir. It would give us, they imagined, a trendy edge over the other kids at school—the ubiquitous Scarlet Johanssons, Brad Pitts and Nicole Kidmans.

Looking film noir was fine for while. It was when we began to *behave* film noir there were problems. We didn't squabble over toys, we brooded and plotted. We used dark desires, we manipulated. We lit the house in chiaroscuro style. We ascended staircases with doppelganger shadows following behind. We had mirrors, lots of them, some reflecting other mirrors, a dizzying view of infinity that, my brother pointed out, served to remind us of the meaninglessness of life. He was eight and looked like Robert Mitchum in *Out of the Past*. It wasn't until my sister (Barbara Stanwyk from *Double Indemnity*) tipped us over, with the

6

Weetabix-kidnap-blackmail episode, that mum and dad realised what a mess they had made.

So I had this face transplant. Celebrity donor from the eighties called Keith Chegwin. It works, don't you think?

I don't blame mum and dad for trying, though. After all, who'd want a world where everyone's genes were from the same film genre?

PRETTY, AIN'T IT?

MRS KALINSKY SPOKE through wreaths of smoke from the cigarette she had permanently cocked at the side of her head. 'This is Alfred.' The fat pampered cat looked up at her. 'He's insured for two grand.' Her long nylon-clad legs made a hissing sound as she crossed and uncrossed them. 'Double if he gets run over.' She stroked the flabby ball of fur. Bars of shadow from the Venetian blinds made her expression unreadable.

But I couldn't go through with it. Then, two weeks later, a ginger tom got flattened on the A556 out of Eccles. I scraped him into a bin bag, dyed him Alfred's colour, and took him to Mrs Kalinsky's vet.

I didn't see Mrs Kalinsky again for weeks and I never got my cut. Then, from the window of the police van, I saw her with the vet in a restaurant, drinking wine. And laughing.

ALL MOD CONS

JAKE INVENTED A prescription glass windscreen for his car so that he could drive without wearing his corrective lenses. He enjoyed the feeling of freedom—no plastic pads digging into his nose—and it had the added advantage that car thieves couldn't drive the vehicle unless they happened to have the same degree of myopia.

Jennifer needed a lift. However, she soon began to complain. She couldn't see, everything was blurred, and to stop herself being sick she had to stick her head out the window like a dog.

'You idiot,' she said to him when he dropped her off.

He wouldn't ring her again. A permanent relationship would mean grinding the windscreen to suit two different people and he could imagine the arguments—it would be the self-cleaning bed sheets saga all over again. He went to bed, turned up the shipping forecast and drifted to sleep.

SNIFFIN' GLUE

SHE FOUND THE new chord off a Joni Mitchell album and it blew her mind. It was a minor with an added ninth, which sounded out of tune at first, but when you got used to the two adjacent semitones ringing against each other, it was a gorgeous dissonance like sweet toothache and it became for her the chord that summed up the aching futility of her life.

Jimmy was tall and scruffy with a leery smile and the use of his dad's black Les Paul. He wound up his fuzzbox all the time and hammered out block chords. When he heard her strumming her minor ninth he said, 'Prog rock shite,' and blasted out Blitzkrieg Bop. She watched as he pounded the low slung guitar, his lips in a curious pout of concentration. Maybe it wasn't what you played but how you played it.

STILL IN BOX

DAN WAS IN the back of the shop gluing the arms back into place on a plastic model of Illya Kuryakin from the *Man from U.N.C.L.E.* TV series, a seven-inch figure identified in his catalogue as supremely collectable and in mint condition, and recently ordered via Dan's web site by a seventies cult TV obsessive from Shard End, when he heard the policeman's voice out the front .

He ignored it and began to unpack the *Phantom Menace* shite. This stuff kept the shop going. But he wished people would pay more attention to his collectable room—his *Starsky & Hutch* section, for example.

'People are disappearing,' he heard the policeman tell his assistant 'This is the second one.' Dan climbed out of the storeroom window and ran up the hill. Why did they always come for him first?

SPEAKING IN PANTONE

VERITY'S LIPS WERE deep coral. More Pantone 667 CV than the wispy Pantone Pink 301 they'd been last month. Pete's skin looked greyer than usual—an almost precise Pantone PMS 428. Coral and grey. Verity and Pete didn't go together. In the Pantone scheme they just didn't match.

Pete wanted a rerun of last month's flyer: FREE DELIVERY WITHIN THREE MILES in balloon extra-bold, over a clip art pizza flying through the air like a frisbee. The soaring pizza with the whizzy motion lines had been my idea and Verity loved it.

'You and your creative juices,' she said. 'You're wasted here.'

I pulled the old leaflet out from its file and winced again when I saw their company motto, squirming along the foot of the flyer in an apologetic script font: QUALITY IS OUR SILENT SALESMAN. The phrase, silent salesman, conjured in my mind some weird, bedsit-dwelling, middle-aged divorcee with few social skills, and felt a tinch creepy. Verity pretended not to understand my point of view. I guess she didn't want to upset Pete, who by now must have noticed our outrageous flirting and overt chemical bonding.

'How many?'

'Make it five thousand,' Pete said. 'We got a good response, didn't we, darling?'

'Well, I don't know, love.' Verity leaned further in towards me across the counter. 'I just do the books, don't I? That's what it says on the papers, doesn't it? Bookkeeper.' She looked at me and winked. 'Not even co-director, or joint-owner. Not even wife. You know what he's described as?' Her crimson fingernails scraped the air in inverted commas. 'Director of Marketing.'

'And Operations.'

'And Operations.' He stroked her face and grinned at her. 'Aawww. Sorry, my pet. You're my biggest asset, you know that.' He narrowed his eyes at me. 'You see, Rick, you don't have many assets in my business. Mopeds. Cheese. Bases. Tomato sauce. Oven. That's it really. Small things, like your family, become very important. That's why we're moving house.'

'Oh, are you?'

'Bramhall.'

'Bit upmarket.'

Verity threw me a larky, conspiratorial smile. 'Classed as Bramhall,'

'Oh.'

'But,' Pete raised his eyebrows, '*classed* as Bramhall, Rick, so you know. Up and up.'

I went round the back and passed the order to the lads. I could hear Verity and Pete arguing, constricted hissy sentences batting to and fro. It was clear they hated each other. Pete had overstretched them with the extra mopeds. Verity was petrified of risk, just like her father. What were they going to eat for the next month? Tacky OVER-SWEET tomato paste? It wasn't *over sweet*. Yes it was, it was cloying, sickly, like treacle.

'There's a problem,' I said when I reappeared, 'with Pantone 678. Can I do them in a different shade?'

'We'll trust you, darling,' Verity said.

13

'I don't give a shit,' said Pete, 'as long as you can read our number.'

'Colour communicates more deeply,' I said. 'You think you are simply reading text but you are being spoken to at a much deeper level, and a truer, more permanent message is imprinted on your mind. Colour has a mainline directly to the soul. See that? Pantone blue 2717C? It speaks of a need— a cold and shivering desire which must be fulfilled, and your phone number—in Pantone orange 021—satisfies that need. It's called anchoring. The satisfaction of that need will be etched in the recesses of the readers' subconsciousness.'

In the back I began to redesign the *printed by* panel on the bottom of the leaflet, the one with my name on it. This one had to be good because I was in real danger of losing her. Classed as Bramhall. Classed as Bramhall was a long way away.

I knew that my name on the leaflet would be the first thing Verity would read. *Rick Thomas* in bold Pantone Rubine Red. Last month it had been Pantone War. I was working up. Every time she looked at it the colour got deeper. As, I hoped, would her love.

DIE LIKE A ROCK

AMY ANALPROBE, LEAD singer of Slime, screamed and leapt from the stage. Everything froze as her body knifed through the air towards me. Her long leg, encased in thigh-high PVC and terminating in a six-inch stiletto, was hurtling towards my right eye.

She had recognised me.

It was my idea. I'd booked the bands to audition for the fictional festival, Punk in the Park. Slime's performance had been a raucous cacophony of annoying juvenilia. 'Plastic Brain' was mildly catchy, 'My Head's on Fire' quite amusing, but all in all, the music, if that's what you called it, failed to take me to any emotional heights. It was not The Floyd or Genesis, that was for sure.

But we'd made a few interesting connections. As well as Amy Analprobe, we'd identified Vincent Vomit, drums with Hoovercock, and Destiny E. Ville, bass for Donny Dark and the Nightmares. The 'challenging' names the musicians had given themselves failed to shock or amuse me. In fact, as far as I and the rest of the DHSS Fraud and Special Investigations Unit were concerned, the whole punk phenomenon was a social construct designed with the specific intention of making fraudulent benefit claims. And our job today was to link these characters with their real life names. They were all, we knew for certain, signing-on at various dole offices whilst earning a packet riding the first wave of punk.

The heel made contact and the pain was searing. Within moments everything went black.

I came round to find my head on Amy Analprobe's lap. We were speeding along in a rattling old van. Amy was stroking me absent-mindedly whilst humming the melody to 'Plastic Brain' softly under her breath. The bin liner she wore as a shirt was stuck to my ear with sweat. I didn't dare move. I could hear the muffled moans of the rest of the fraud team, tied up in the back. My head hurt, but luckily she'd missed my eye.

'Is he still out?' I heard the van driver say.

'Yeh,' she said, 'but let's not hurt him.'

'There's no other way. He'll have to be put with the others.'

'No. I like this one. I want to keep him. Can I keep him, please?'

I opened an eye and saw through the windscreen a dark country road, white lines flashing towards us, a big fat full moon high up in the sky.

GREAT INVENTIONS # 1

MY GRANDFATHER CAN remember the days before train doors were invented. At that time trains rushed about the country—up, down and across—stopping at platforms for a clean and a change of driver, their carriages empty, their seating clean and pristine, their floors unscuffed. It cost a lot to run them, and the government was at a point of closing down the whole network when one day a little girl climbed down from a cleaning platform in Runcorn and wriggled though a small hole into a carriage. She sat on the seat and when the train arrived at Liverpool she emerged onto the platform, unscathed.

Little Lucy Marshall had invented train doors.

And who can now imagine doing without them? They've become part of everyday life and we walk on and off a train without even giving them a second thought.

LUCKY WINNER

I CAN MOVE round this shop quicker than you would think, so when he grabbed the Hula Hoops and legged it for the door, I was there before him. He was a decent guy, though. He apologised, he'd got no vouchers, no hostel, nothing, and I said, don't worry, eat them. So he wolfed them down and handed me the empty packet. And that's when I saw the winning ticket at the bottom. I didn't know what to do. It was his prize by rights. We carried on chatting. Officially he didn't exist. His lawyer had taken him to the end of the line and now he was down for deportation, but they couldn't take him because Iraq's a no-fly zone. So he was a non-person and got no support at all.

I'll be honest, I didn't give him the prize. Tickets to the Stereophonics. I thought he'd suffered enough.

A GOOD DEAL

WE WERE ON the train and Lindsey had been gassing into her phone for ages. 'That was Carl,' she said, 'He's in the Mona Lisa of bad fake Oirish pubs.'

'He rang just to chat?'

'Yeh.' She made crocodile jaws with her hand and snapped them together. 'I've never had a man like it.'

'Unfuckingbelievable.'

'Well,' she smiled wistfully into the mobile as if Carl was peering out at her, 'he got a good deal—Orange, thirty hours off-peak free. So...'

'So he uses it.'

She spun the clamshell Siemens on the table and we watched the blurred propeller until it stopped. 'He'd ring anyway. What deal's Frankie on?'

I turned my Nokia upside down and stroked its shining steel curves. 'Cellnet, Pay As You Go.'

'And does he ring?'

'He texts.'

A phone on the next table pinged and our hands whipped to the handsets like cowboys rushing to draw.

THROUGH THE MEDIUM OF
MODERN DANCE

THE BIN MEN laid out the recycling boxes and pressed play. Latin beats spluttered out and from a wheelie bin sprang a woman in floaty clothes. She danced as she demonstrated how to recycle. A bin man battered hell out of a bongo.

Within every bottle are pieces of all the bottles you've ever used, they sang

The dancer had long ochre hair. Freckles. She hated *Newsnight* and laminate flooring. She liked celeriac. And ferris wheels.

She was my ex-girlfriend.

My insides churned with recalled desire and when she'd finished I gripped her arm. But she pointed at the label on a tin: DO NOT REHEAT.

When we lived together *I* dealt with the rubbish; a monstrous heap of unloved packaging and decayed food. We threw away more than we ever ate. It was better when everything got burnt. Ash men came with an ash cart and grey flecks wheeled in the air, getting in our eyes.

GREAT INVENTIONS # 2

BEFORE GEORGE LEVIN invented people who can't fight back, everybody could fight back. You had to be careful what you said. But in 1931 Levin developed several prototype people who can't fight back and these individuals were sent out to settle in the community. They multiplied and soon there was a whole section of the population that you could say or do anything to and they wouldn't—or couldn't—retaliate. People who can't fight back are taken for granted nowadays, but think back to those days and imagine what it was like. We owe it to pioneers like Levin for maintaining the peaceful and harmonious society we enjoy today.

SMALLER THAN ONE-EIGHTIETH THE DIAMETER OF A HUMAN HAIR

I'M BIG IN little things, things smaller than one-eightieth the diameter of a human hair. I love the job, it suits me, but Janice isn't impressed and when I got an invite to present a poster at the Micro5 conference in Iceland she went into her usual rant. What's so absolutely fascinating about things that are below a certain size? A dog might be the same size as a sewing machine, but does that give them something in common?

It was good in Iceland to share time with other people who were passionate about things smaller than one-eightieth the diameter of a human hair. I met Helen on the hot springs trip. 'You know how I explain to my students the length of a nanometre?' she told me. 'It's the amount my pubes grow every second.'

The next day Helen and I sat close together watching the final presentation. The lecturer was a pony-tailed boffin whose tie looked like it had been dipped in batter. I drew a picture of him with a Burger King crown on his head, wheels for legs, and a speech bubble that said *I am a twat*. We laughed, really, really laughed. All around us everyone was thinking about things that were smaller than one-eightieth the diameter of a human hair, and the room seemed to hum with promise. For the first time in ages I didn't feel like

I was a tiny particle being examined through a microscope by higher beings in a laboratory.

BLURRED GIRLS

GUS WORKED AT the photolab for years before I discovered his secret. Pinned all over the shed wall, dozens of blurred images of women.

Weeks later we were making love and he abruptly stopped, rolled over, and sighed. 'I'm sorry. It's just, I wish you were more, I don't know—blurred. Maybe if you let me wear these?' He produced a pair of massive square spectacles with jam jar lenses. Behind them his eyes swam in a murky grey pool. 'They belonged to my mother.'

It was as if a gorgeous piece of jewellery were being handed down. I wanted to crush these spectacles. They staring up at me reproachfully, like the picked out eyes of a great monster, made me feel synthetic, a spectral image on scratched glass. But destroying them was impossible. They were the prism through which Gus loved me.

I tried to accommodate his wishes, but over time his obsession grew too difficult to bear. In the shed the collection had grown. A dim aquarium of blurred girls all innocent of their place in his sick museum. I made a bonfire and threw the blurred photos on to it.

His feet pounded up the stairs and I was sure he would kill me. Everything seemed in slow motion and far away, a melting sugar-glass land. But Gus wasn't angry. He agreed with what I'd done. Pictures were unhealthy. It was then he told me we weren't alone. He'd brought back some friends, friends of the same *persuasion*. Would I mind if they looked at me through their spectacles? He'd told them how wonderful I was when I was blurred. They were at the bottom of the stairs, hungrily staring up through huge, thick glasses.

They followed me meekly to the shed and once inside I gave them cereal and milk. Then I locked the padlock.

My new man likes everything in sharp focus. An airline pilot. He barbeques too, and at the end of a summer evening we like to gather with our friends around the shed window to watch the men inside drinking chocolate milk and gawping at their blurred pictures. We could never live like that, yet we feel a small portion of envy; the simple way they look up when we coo at them through the speakers, and the way they sleep, all together on the floor, curled up like cashews.

THE SECRET PICTURES
OF DAVID CAMERON

DANNY AND GILL asked us to stay at their house whilst they went to Budapest. They needed some time alone, to sort a few things out, get some perspective. Lately, the whole routine had been getting them down. Work, sleep, work, sleep; like living in cement. They were going to take life by the scruff of its neck and shake it.

We'd dropped them at the airport, raced back, and were about to settle down to a DVD on Danny's giant plasma TV with surround sound, when the new Tory leader, David Cameron, appeared on the news. And we noticed that he was the spitting image of Danny; the same moonish face, the same eager, slightly brittle expression, the same springy, puppy-dog gait. Pundits wagered Cameron would run to fat, and we'd said exactly the same about Danny.

So when Danny rang from Budapest to remind us to switch off the electronic timer for his lawn sprinkler system, Adelle asked him straight away if he knew that he looked exactly, precisely, *uncannily*, like David Cameron.

Ray protested violently, and Adelle couldn't understand why. After all, Cameron was fairly handsome, in his Converse All Stars and faded jeans—even a bit fanciable, if you allowed Tories a sexual dimension. But I understood. Danny was unutterably pompous about his Trotskyite past, flogging

Socialist Worker in the stabbing cold, agitating for the student hard left. The fact that a famous Tory looked just like him reminded him of how far he had betrayed his socialist roots—shares in multi-nationals, job in global pharmaceuticals, private school lined up for the offspring.

It was hilarious. So the night before he was due back I printed out dozens of smarmy publicity shots of Cameron. We sought out unusual and surprising sites for our poster campaign: under the toilet seat, inside cupboard doors, the bottom of the bread bin, beneath the dried food in the cat's bowl, inside a cereal box, under pillows, the bottom of Gill's underwear drawer. The one at the base of the sugar bowl was a real slow burner. The pictures were everywhere and the next day we left the house exhilarated by our grand joke, looking forward to the irritated but amused phone call we would receive from Danny.

But the call we got the following evening was from Gill, and it wasn't like that at all. She'd returned alone. Danny had left her. He'd been seeing someone else. It had gone on for quite some time. Now, she couldn't get his face out of her mind. His lying, cheating, shit-eating smile. In fact, she'd got a bit angry, smashed a few things up. But we shouldn't worry. She'd been about to redecorate, anyway. Starting with the hall. The hall is the most important place, didn't I agree?

I put down the phone and picked up my car keys. I looked at our own hall. Gill was right; a hall should always be decorated first. A hall is where the private and public worlds meet. If the hall isn't right, nothing's going to work.

THE NEWT LADY'S
DEAD NOW

IT WAS NO coincidence that the deep-fried goats' cheese shaped like a windmill reminded Henry McNally of where he lost his virginity with Two-Bag Marion, the school technician. Henry was eating from the special menu, a three-course experience designed to reach down into the deepest recess of your soul.

My regular diners told me it was the little things they appreciated, not just the food. The way I remembered personal details and incorporated them into their evening. This led me to develop the personalised menu service.

Each meal took a lot of research. Hiding in bushes, sifting through bins, following people into pubs, bugging phones. But the results were worth it. The name *Natasha* spelled out in scarlet on a lamb cutlet would help begin the healing process for the cheated-on Mrs MacFarlane, and the mottled-green jelly desert I prepared for Hilary Bostock would reminded her of the old newt lady who imprisoned her for an hour and seventeen minutes when she was nine.

Often the diners cried as they were eating, the tears mingling with the sauces. Now and again they argued and left the restaurant separately. Sometimes they didn't seem to appreciate the little things I'd done. One couple tipped the food on to the floor and stamped it into the carpet. The room was deathly quiet when they had finished. All you could hear was the couple breathing heavily and, from outside, the automated voice on our courtesy minibus saying 'this vehicle is reversing' over and over again.

THE LIFE OF RILEY

THE GUARD POINTED at Maureen's shoes. 'Gotta take the laces, cutie. Three swingers this year already.'

Hours elongated into days, time became geological. The continent buckled and stretched beneath her. Would she see cheeky Hannah and wee Jack again? She thought back to Ian's grinning face on the Kwik Save security tape: Yogi Bear mask dangling about his neck, everyone in the courtroom cackling.

Judge Noon was a progressive thinker who delighted in experiments. After all, who would suffer the most? Ian Gillespie? In prison? A warm sleep, regular meals, no worries about the electric or the social? Or Maureen Gillespie, dragging up two kids on her own? He made a radical decision. Maureen would serve the time and Ian would stay outside.

It was cold. She couldn't remember whether summer was ending or spring beginning. The educational programme looked interesting. Film studies. This year was the gangster genre.

YOU'VE CHOSEN TO BE EXCITED

AUDREY FLAILED AROUND the dance floor, gnashing and gurning to the bleeps and hi-hat sniffs, doing big-fish-little-fish-cardboard-box, but I was unable to join her. Each time I activated my clubbing implant the management-consultancy implant kicked in as well. So along with the usual wave of ecstasy—my whole body a quivering erogenous zone—came a rushing urge to produce a tabular action plan. The type of psychic-leakage I'd worried about on the bus back from Aldi.

The saw rasped as the Aldi doctor re-opened the entry flap. 'These babies may not be known brands,' he said, speaking softly, as if my open skull were a cathedral, 'but they're by the same companies.' On the screen a spiked instrument appeared, jabbing at grey jelly, cells sparking and fizzing like an electric storm. The tyre kick of the brain surgeon. 'Some synaptic smearing,' he said. 'I can sort that out. . . .' While I'm in here, do you want to try the new desire patch? Not the actual one, but quality lookey-likey.'

Six months later Audrey explained to the Judge how I was unable to make love unless the bed was full of Airfix models, and he agreed this was distressing. I mentioned the cheap supermarket brain implants, but he wouldn't listen. Audrey got the kids, the house, everything.

31

It wasn't long before the Aldi doctor rang, from California. He'd paid for their flights. He was sorry it had come to this. All's fair, as they say. But I was unable to get upset. The Asda implants I'd had to counteract the Aldi ones made me see everything in a pink fuzzy light. Quite pleasant, really.

GREAT INVENTIONS # 3

THE GREATEST INVENTION of all was the invention of edges. Before the invention of edges, nothing had an end— or for that matter a start. Objects like waste paper bins or key rings or pavements didn't end—they blurred into each other. Even people didn't have edges. You simply flowed into other people, so you didn't really know where your wife or friend or father started or began, or even what the difference was between a toaster and your cousin, things were blended in so well. When, in 1974, Dr. Ralph Morrin invented edges, the most difficult task was to decide where to place the edges of the objects that Dr. Morrin had defined as intrinsically separate to each other. The 1974 Edge Committee was established to arbitrate on where the cuts between objects were to be made—decisions we live with to this day. Despite some ongoing disputes about whether the new edges were placed correctly in the first place, it is accepted by most people that a world without edges would be a poorer place—it's hard to imagine how we ever did without them!

ARE WE ROMPING NOW?

MY GREAT-GRANDDAD USED to describe them to me, going all misty-eyed as he spoke of the variety of shapes, the elaborate apparel to conceal and support, and the dozens of slang names. He spoke in detail about several pairs he'd actually touched.

Now we have no use for them. Extra-uterine wombs, chemical transgender pills and the long goodbye to utility sex meant society ceased to find them sexually attractive. That first rush of accelerated evolution saw them off in two generations and eventually even silicone implants were passé. Yet were we happy? It seemed to me that when sex became fun, all the fun was bled out of it.

I looked at Julia where she stood, naked before the mirror. It was true. What had begun as tiny pillows of fat had developed into a huge heaving bosom. She'd been hiding it from everyone, strapping herself into a tight girdle. The sight opened up a culvert to a greasy, antique world of nervy synthesiser riffs, lime spandex trouser suits, breathless heels.

'What will we do?' I said.

'I can't imagine,' she said. 'But at least now we know.'

I looked at her. 'Know?'

'Which one of us would have been the woman. It's a little annoying. I thought I was being so good—washing, cooking, nurturing. I had a feeling I was working against type.'

I went across and put my arm over her shoulder. 'Go on,' I said. 'Give us a feel.'

CLOWN TIME IS OVER

When I was a kid I met a clown. We were walking back from Cleator Moor carnival and he caught up with us, me and Brissy, and asked the way to Jacktrees Road. It was raining hard, smashing down in rods, and he's still in all his make-up and this big orange wig and he tells us there's a woman he knows on Jacktrees Road and he might just look in on her while he's here in town. Up close he's really old, and he has this fierce bad smell, what with the rain and everything, like years and years of dried sweat had been released from his costume in one go. He had a gut on him like he'd swallowed a small deer.

So there we were, two kids walking along with a clown. I remember thinking if this was an Enid Blyton story we'd have been delighted; he would have been a felt-pen coloured, jolly old buffer, folding balloons and plucking coins from behind our ears. But walking with him wasn't like that. It was frightening. He talked all the time, in a reckless headlong way, about how he used to be chairman of some national clown club and how it wasn't the same anymore, it had become too Americanised. You couldn't even sit a kid on your knee anymore, he complained. He repeated this several times like having a kid on his knee was the most important thing about the profession.

We reached Jacktrees Road and he said goodbye and I remember wondering if he really knew a woman on that road, and what would she have thought to open her door and find a soaking wet clown there?

I work as a doctor now, and it's part of my job to give people bad news. And when you have to deliver awful information, such as informing a wife that her husband is dead, or a father that his daughter's leg will be amputated, a common nervous reaction is a powerful desire to laugh out loud. At medical school we used to practise giving bad news all the time, and we had to devise methods to avoid this happening, and the method I used was to picture that wet clown, walking up that street towards that woman's house, his long shoes flapping and his wig jiggling up and down. I see the clown walking up the street and I hear the words coming out of my mouth and everything—my tone, my posture, my facial expression—is perfect for that moment in time. I can only say that we should all thank our good god in heaven for sending us clowns for that reason alone.

THE ACCUSED MADE
SPIDER FURNITURE

LITTLE THINGS ARE little for a reason. They are little because they are unimportant. Little people, for example. They don't get served at the bar, they go unnoticed in restaurants, slip by invisible on the street. They are little because they have grown to fit the space they deserve, no more than that. But this isn't a problem. All we need to do is put the little people in charge of little things and big people will take care of the big things. Little people will manage drawing pins, matches, watch batteries and earrings. They will manufacture bicycles for travelling insect shows. Big people will control the cars, the trucks, the buildings, and the jet planes. The problem is guns. Guns are small but I wouldn't let little people have guns. Little people run amok if given guns. A gun makes a little person complete.

CONTAINER DRIVER

IT WAS A last minute cancellation, so one day we're in a travel agents, the next frying in coconut oil under a saturated blue sky. But I couldn't relax.

'I can't stop thinking,' I said, 'about the people who cancelled. The bloke was a container driver, like the ones who drop off at the yard.'

She looked blank.

'Heart attack. Smashed through the central reservation.'

She squeezed her eyes against the sun. 'Don't think about it.'

'This is his holiday. We should go home.'

She didn't agree. So we trailed round the market, the pearl factory, the melon farm, the barbeque, neither of us with the heart for it.

'I wonder what he would have thought of it,' I said.

'The container driver?'

'Yes.'

'I don't think he'd have liked it,' she said

'He'd have bloody hated it,' I said, and began to dance to the pulse of the Bontempi organ.

USING THE FACILITIES

WE CAME HOME to find a fat bloke sat on the toilet, his trousers round his ankles, reading a paper and chortling.

'It says here,' he said, 'that some bloke swallowed a live snake and it lived inside him for years.'

'What are you doing in my house?'

He folded the paper and rested it on his bare thighs 'Day out?'

'Who are you, exactly?'

'Keswick again, I bet. You've been to Keswick five times this year. Chips from Fry Ups?'

'What do you want?'

'The Crown does chips.' He smacked his leg with the rolled newspaper. 'Plate of, two pounds. But you never bother. However, you use The Crown's facilities all the time. Waltz in, straight to the bogs, never mind you haven't bought anything, or contributed to the upkeep of the lavatories. Well, I'm the landlord.' He stood and pulled his trousers up. 'And now you know how it feels.'

CHAIRS MISSING

THEY USED TO talk to each other. About loose leg joints, fraying seat covers, unsatisfactory positions in the room. About how one wasn't used enough, how one was sat on by the heaviest resident, how the Crowther boy habitually rubbed the back of one with greasy fingers causing a pale shiny pate like a bald head. They discussed Mrs O'Neil, with her old-fashioned dusting technique and cheap polish that smelt of rancid fat.

But they couldn't speak anymore. They had forgotten how. They stood in silence, able to communicate only by gesture, and only one gesture at that—the gesture of open arms, which said, 'Come fill this empty space, I am waiting for you, only you,' and the sad fact is that this was not what any of them wanted to say at anytime, not what they wanted to say at all.

SHOOTING LULU

WITH MILLIONS OF pounds to manage and hundreds of lives under his control, I couldn't imagine how Geoff coped.

'What do you do,' I asked him, 'on days when you feel everything's spiky and triangular? Or when you can communicate in only high-pitched shouting?'

Geoff stopped and extracted a cigarette from its packet.

'Or when you hate everyone's eyes? Or when everything sounds like growling?'

He lit the cigarette. 'What are you doing in my garden, Darren?'

I put my face close to his and spoke in Lulu's voice. 'I need to learn how to relax, Geoff.'

He moved away and nodded at his wheelbarrow, spilling over with mangled shrubs. 'This is how I chill out.'

'But I'm a cleaner. This kind of work is what I do for a job.'

Later, I watched him through my binoculars, tossing leaves onto the compost heap. I pictured barbed fangs on the inside of his clothes that ripped his flesh as he moved.

This helped.

A FEEL FOR FORMAT

IT WAS TIME for the hilarious anecdote and I was going to give my I-got-married-dressed-as-Elvis routine with the 8x10 to back it up, but this producer wasn't going for it. So I told him, if it was good enough for Strike it Lucky, I think it'll work here, on what was, I reminded him, a school-run filler for cable. I *know* game shows. 'Andy, you treat the camera like a friend,' Tarrant once said, 'and that can't be learnt.' It's true I have something special. It's a feel, a feel for format.

Then this producer starts asking about hobbies and I told him: 'Game shows, game shows are my life.' Then he says that they won't need me after all. They want people who are more real.

'When did I cease to be real?' I say.

'Judging by your CV,' he says, 'somewhere between *Fifteen to One* and *Family Fortunes*.'

GROCKEL BASHING

WE CALL THEM grockels round here. Holiday people, people who wear shorts when the weather's shite, push prams with buckets and spades hanging off them, and sit on the beach when its mortal cold. Grockel bashing was my idea.

The first one was a fat bloke with massive Eric Morecambe shorts carrying a bag of pop for his kids. We tripped him up outside Boots and pelted him with seaweed. Next was a woman with three kids. We told her this empty garage was where you bought flying swing tokens, then locked them in for four hours. Then we pushed this little bloke with nine ice creams into a load of shell ornaments, smashing the lot.

The tourist board are saying it's wrong, slagging us off on the news, moaning that it's damaging trade, but what do they know? My dog was killed by a grockel and don't forget it.

CLEANING UP NEW YORK

'PAY ATTENTION TO the little things,' Mayor Giuliani said, his face bobbing up and down on two huge screens as he strode about the conference stage describing how he cleaned up late-eighties New York. 'The little things are key.'

So I went home and immediately began to apply Giuliani's theory to my own life. Elsie hated that I consumed five and a half cans of Guinness and eight different pills each night, and that I took old girlfriends away for weekends. She hated that I ran the pit bull fights down the Railway, wore cheap green clothes, and had lizardy eyes. But I couldn't do anything about any of those things. But what I could do was sort out the little things. I had the habit of dipping my fingers in the hummus then opening the fridge without wiping my hands, so I stopped doing that. I used to say, 'Christ save me from this banality,' every time Dido came on the TV, so I stopped doing that as well.

After a week I asked her if she'd noticed an improvement and she looked at me with an amazed expression on her face. Was I on the same planet? I was a bastard pig who cared only for himself.

I would have to confront Mayor Giuliani.

Giuliani opened the door to his hotel room and looked at me for a long time. His face trembled and water appeared in his eyes.

'It hasn't worked for me,' I said. 'Your little things method.'

He beckoned me into the bedroom where his wife was sleeping. He shook her shoulder with some urgency and when she sat up, he passed her a pair of spectacles.

'It's Terry,' he said to her. 'He's come home.'

AROMABINGO

DODGING A STEEL dart squealing through the air whilst maintaining the lotus position is not easy and today, owing probably to a late night and over-indulgence on the red wine front, Hilary didn't get out of the way. The tungsten point slashed a stripe of red across her cheek, and she screamed and leapt up.

The thrower, short and plump, looked beadily about him, then planted his lager on the gym floor and ambled across

'I'm sorry, lady. Forgot the rubber safety tip.' He had a wheedling, tinny voice. 'But when you're sitting at double-top you've got to expect a few well-aimed shots.'

'Oh, I'm so very, very sorry,' Hilary said. Her sarcasm hung in the air like fog.

She was sick of it. *Darts 'n' yoga night*, another noxious inter-class cohesion strategy, like the canal full of fish with poems on their bellies to get young working-class men reading again.

'Here.' The man pressed a handkerchief against her face. He smelt of cheap, sweaty gold and warmed-up nylon. 'You don't want to get it infected. Let's take you to get some first aid.'

In the cupboard they kissed. Outside, she could hear the darts team chatting away, their deep voices congealing in the echoing gym into a dissonant, growling choir.

47

PART TWO

TWELVE-INCH SINGLES

THE HAPPINESS WELL

O'DONNALL TOOK ME to Pontoon Four where the accident happened. It was the first time I'd been to the well. The substance in the steel liner was exactly the colour I expected—luminous cornflower yellow—but the consistency was not the blobby, custard-like goo I'd imagined as a child. It was disappointingly thin, like a consommé.

O'Donnall showed me where he'd slipped in, pointing to the loose perimeter rail, now cordoned off with danger tape. Finger scrapes in the slime on the edges of the tank indicated where his fingernail was torn off in his panic to escape. I looked at his hand, the bandaged finger.

The dark brown cloud O'Donnall caused to appear in the well was now a brooding presence in the middle of the yellow pond. Over on another pontoon, a group of men in suits and fluorescent waistcoats looked worried. Chins were stroked, heads were shook, curses muttered. One man was taking photographs. Another had a long pole which he prodded into the centre of the dark misty shape as if it might change something.

My job was to find out three things: how it had happened, why O'Donnall had been allowed to work at the well whilst he was unhappy, and how to put things right.

I leaned on the rail and listened to O'Donnall as he explained. A slight Cumbrian accent flavoured his sentences, lending his conversation a jolly, rural feel. I could see how he had got away with it for so long.

He'd been ashamed of how he felt and kept putting off telling his local area coordinator. One of the reasons he hadn't told anyone was because he was three-fifths of the way through a community samba coaching course that he'd waited five years to join. Samba tutors were well respected in his local area forum and he had wanted to do this ever since he was a child. But he knew that the people at the local area activity hub wouldn't wish to have a depressed man teaching samba drumming. Consequently, no one but O'Donnall himself knew how miserable he felt. And because his shift supervisor didn't know, he had not been removed from his duties at the well. O'Donnall hadn't realised how important it was that unhappy people didn't contaminate the contents of the pond. He hadn't, until now, comprehended the enormity of the predicament

The brown stain seemed to grow darker as we stared at it. Newspapers had been saying it was expanding, and they appeared to be right. Light brown feelers crept out from its centre into the yellow liquor around it. Since its inception, near the edge where O'Donnall fell in, it had floated into the middle, but it was now moving towards the edge again, and getting close to a little scarf of bubbles which O'Donnall explained was the main outlet pipe. I looked at the structures around the pond. Dozens of tubes and pipes climbed over each other up and out through to the monitoring and distribution centres. Arrows indicated the direction of flow. Beneath us the main feed pipe throbbed as it topped up the pond from deep in the earth.

I made some diagrams and asked a few questions of the other men. Then I asked O'Donnall to take me to the distribution room. Amidst control desks bristling with knobs, levers and slide controls, he explained how each monitor and distributor managed over a hundred individuals, and how sudden surges in demand such as a new born baby, new job, or new relationship meant they constantly had to reduce the flow to other members of the community. The main job of the monitor and distributor was to maintain equilibrium, wherever possible.

~

Back home I sat in the kitchen tent and looked at the diagrams. I could hear my ex-wife reading stories to the foster children in the tent next door. My step-mother-in-law was sitting on the tent floor, playing with the new kittens—six of them, all waiting to be allocated homes. One of the kittens, a fat creature with a sneaky, sarcastic face, scampered over to me and nipped at my bare toes. I reached down and stroked its head while I thought about the well and the dark menacing shape waiting to engulf us, like the cold shadow of a continent.

I decided to make a model. A washing-up bowl represented the steel liner and plastic drinking straws stood in for pipes. Over the next few evenings I worked on the model, perfecting it and perfecting it. Every now and then I rang O'Donnall to clarify aspects of its construction. It had to be right, because this was the most important job that I had ever undertaken. Soon I had a scale model of the plant. I filled it with yellow paint thinned with turpentine and allowed this to settle for a while. Then I spilled in a blob of treacle and watched its behaviour as it floated on the surface. It wasn't long before the treacle insinuated itself into the yellow paint.

I crossed the community garden and went to the phone tent where I rang and left a message for O'Donnall. He rang me an hour later.

'Where have you been?'

'I've started a new samba group. One of my own.'

'But you've only done three-fifths of the training.'

'The important three-fifths. Don't worry.'

I hung up. O'Donnall was useless. He didn't understand what he'd done.

I returned to my tent to find my second cousin waiting outside for me with a letter from the well company.

I read the letter slowly, on my own, with the television off and the radio on low.

After it sunk in, I placed the letter on my lap and looked out of the open tent flap, over to the community bar. No music could be heard, no laughter, no shouting, no clack of pool balls, no din from the heavy metal band that sometimes rehearsed there. The well company had stopped everything in their efforts to head off a surge. I imagined that in every local area forum, in every tent, people were sitting alone, thinking about the well, and the creeping, spreading stain.

I went into the kitchen tent. My step-mother-in-law was feeding the kittens with their special kitten food and I watched her for a time. I could hear my ex-wife in the next door tent reading stories to the foster children, the same stories she always read.

I looked back at the model; the yellow water was completely black.

I left the kitchen tent and went in to the tent next door. The foster children looked up at me. They were surprised to see me in their tent at this time of day. My ex-wife read stories, never me.

'I want to read the stories tonight,' I said and took the book from my ex-wife's hand. 'Please.'

'Isn't he rude, girls,' my ex-wife said.

'Sorry,' I said. 'But tonight, I need to read.'

'But you don't know how to read, Mr Flash,' one of the foster children piped up. 'You can't do the voices.'

'I certainly can,' I said, in a low growly bear's voice, which made them laugh.

My ex-wife raised her eyebrows, then smiled and left the room.

I selected a pile of books from the floor and set them on my knee. 'Tonight I am going to read to you every single storybook in the tent,' I said.

'Mr Flash! Mr Flash! Yes, yes, yes. Thank you, Mr Flash. But don't we have to go to sleep?'

'You can go to sleep whenever you want to, but I will carry on reading the stories and you will still hear them, even while your asleep. So you'll have nice dreams about stories and magic lands.'

'I like those dreams.'

'Okay, then.'

I began to read. I read *Postman Pat*, *Burglar Bill*, *The Three Billy Goats Gruff*, everything. I read and read, doing all the voices and sound effects that I could manage. My pace grew faster and faster and the pages whipped through my fingers. Soon the foster children were fast sleep, but I carried on reading. I became happier and happier the more I read. I was dizzy, drunk with joy. I imagined the poor monitors and distributors back at the well trying to balance the supply, and the dark stain moving inexorably towards the scarf of bubbles around the outlet pipe.

When I'd read every single book I returned to the kitchen tent and played with the kittens. I would play and play until the kittens and I were completely exhausted.

LAST CHANCE TO
TURN AROUND

SHE'D BEEN COMING every Saturday for months. Late for-ties, right age for the hey-day, had some of the moves as well, a few slides and a nifty shuffle on the back-beat. She asked for the right records, often flipped through my box nodding at some rare disc. Faintly sneered, I thought, when I played something off a CD collection, but danced to it any-way. The bloke she came with was younger, a lot younger I would say. He wouldn't know what Wigan Casino had been about, why people sewed patches on to their hold-alls, why they chucked talcum powder over the floor.

This particular night she had been acting strangely. Kept her jacket on and hadn't danced, just sat nodding her head to the beat. She was on her own too—no boyfriend in tow.

At the end of my session the landlord gave me a wink and we got a lock in. I stuck on a compilation and sat down next to her.

'Where's Blondie?'

'Blondie's gone.'

She sipped her Becks, then produced a paper package from her pocket. 'See this? I've been meaning to give you it for years.'

I raised my eyebrows, took the package from her and peeled away the paper. I couldn't believe my eyes. An ancient forty-five, big rarity on the scene—Tobi Legend, 'Time Will Pass You By'.

'You want me to play it for you?'

'No, it's yours.'

'I can't take it. It's worth something, you know.'

'No, I mean it belongs to you. Nineteen seventy-three? Twisted Wheel? You gave it to me.'

Something about the way she sipped her beer struck a chord and I suddenly remembered. 'I'm sorry. I was young, stupid.'

'You've been on my mind lately, that's all. You get to thinking.'

'I know. Mid-life stuff.'

The hole in the centre of the disc became a time-tunnel, sucking me down thirty swirling years. You flip things over and over in your head and wonder what might have happened. We sat and soaked in the songs till the landlord chucked us out.

~

I got on the back of her Vespa and soon the gaudy lights of the Rusholme curry mile melted into leafy Whalley Range and we were outside her house.

The room was cold and smelt vaguely of warm milk.

'In there.'

She flicked on the light to reveal an Aladdin's cave of Northern Soul. Giant soul icons frowned down from the walls and the floor was stacked with vinyl 45s. Teetering towers of books—*Casino Magic*, *Keep The Faith*, *Wigan Dreams*, everywhere you looked soul, soul, soul. Strangest of all was a structure by the far wall, which I could only describe as an altar. She went straight over to it and beckoned me to follow.

'This is my special place.'

I joined her in front of her shrine. On the floor was a cushion and there was a rail to put your elbows. A small tabernacle in the centre of the altar was obscured by a velvet curtain, and she tugged a cord. It slid across to reveal an old publicity photograph of me.

I stopped breathing for a few moments, and she turned and smiled

'You're a bit younger in that one, but it's all I could find. Snipped it out of *Soul and Blues* magazine. Every evening I put on the 'Three After Midnight' and think back to those times.'

This woman was one dog-faced boy short of a freak show.

'Can I use your facilities?'

She motioned me to a door at the back of the room. Inside I found a small toilet, a basin and, weirdly, a low bed like a little cot. Some kind of granny flat. Then the door clicked and a bolt scraped across.

I looked for an escape route. There was a window, a tiny little square of glass at head height. I tried to peer through, but a sheet of paper had been stuck over the outside. I stared harder; I was looking at the back of my photograph. The picture was ripped away and a middle-aged woman genuflected shyly then knelt on the plump velour cushion. Her arms drooped over the rail and she tilted her head. The muffled chords of a soul ballad throbbed.

I lay down on the bed and looked at the wall. Nothing to do, nowhere to go. Just this, endless this. There was a flap at the bottom of the door. That's how she would send in my food. Later I would sit at the little window again. I could tell when she wanted me to sit at the window and when to stay on the bed. At last I could relax. I could act my age.

YOU AND YOU ALONE

ANGELA AND ROWAN loved each other. Utterly, thoroughly, completely. All was love. Angela was crammed to the brim with pulsating pink jelly; Rowan was on a speeding motorbike screeching down a long curving road.

But there were small imperfections; a fraction of time when the speeding motorbike shuddered and gasped, a tiny fissure in the pink jelly. And the cause of these wrinkles were the ex-lovers. Neither Angela nor Rowan were young, so over the years they had collected an assortment of ex-wives, husbands, boyfriends, and girlfriends. Not to mention the many flings, flirtations and encounters they had each enjoyed. Although they rarely met any of the exs, the knowledge of their existence and of the intimacies their partner had shared with these strangers oppressed them. At night Angela would wake up and imagine she could see the ex-lovers swaggering up and down in front of her, pointing and laughing. Rowan said he sometimes felt as though he was lying under many thick, heavy blankets, and the blankets were all the exs.

This went on. Dark cavities appeared in the pink jelly. The speeding motorbike coughed and puttered, threatening to stall.

Something had to be done, and the solution was simple. They would kill all of their ex-lovers. When the ex-lovers were dead, the couple would be utterly content and it would be jelly and motorbikes wall to wall.

They agreed on the definition of an ex—you had to have slept with them more than once, spent a whole night together, and shared drinks or food. This criteria helped reduce the list, but there were still a lot of people to kill.

They agreed that Rowan would kill her exes and Angela would kill his. That way it would be harder for the police to trace the murderers. And to make it even more difficult to connect these suspicious deaths—twenty-six in total—each of the killings would be carried out differently. Rowan listed the various ways available and matched the victim with the method, based on his knowledge of that person's preferences. A certain ex-lover hated water, so drowning was out. Another was afraid of heights, so the push off the cliff was not possible. Someone hated blood, so the knife was not an option. One had a fear of being buried alive, so suffocation would be unkind. On a big sheet of paper they worked out a detailed plan which indicated the dates of each of the ex-lover's deaths. Next to the date of completion Angela drew a big pink star and scribbled the word *hurray*.

Six months later the ex-lovers were all dead. It was summer and Angela and Rowan were sitting on their patio holding hands and drinking sparkling wine.

'Are you full of pink jelly?' he asked her

She was.

And was he speeding round the bend on his motorbike?

He gripped invisible handlebars in his fists. '*Vroom, vroom.*'

There they sat in the gathering twilight thinking about what they had achieved. It had gone well. It had been hard work, unpleasant often, but all in all, worth doing. Their world was now perfect.

They began to discuss what had happened to their ex-lovers' bodies after they were killed. Three had been buried (Angela and Rowan attended one of the services) but they had no idea what had happened to the others. Apart from one, who had made it known that he wished his ashes to be shot into space in a small capsule. His new wife had loved him deeply and was certain to have made this happen. His name was Roger Farringdon. The capsule containing his ashes would be circling the earth now, even as they spoke. Angela and Rowan looked up at the sky. It was a clear night and stars were twinkling. It bothered them that Roger Farringdon was up there, spinning in space. It was as if Roger Farringdon still had power over them, as if he was looking down on them, laughing. Typical of a man to want to live forever. They scoured the sky for evidence of the capsule, and after a time imagined that they could see a tiny pinprick reflected off the moon, drifting balletically. As they watched this speck of light circling the earth a thousand miles up, abruptly they felt powerless. Was it only Roger Farringdon? How many of the other ex-lovers had chosen this option? They didn't know. It could be more than one.

What should they do? Suddenly the sky was full of dead souls, strange-eyed constellations looking down on them, mocking their puny lives. The jelly inside her trembled as though it were about to melt. The motorbike slowed down.

There was work to be done, and the options were clear. It was love or the universe—one of them had to go.

ONLY THE STONES
REMAIN

THE DRONE INSIDE me dropped an octave as the mainframe flipped to standby. I could hear Garfield locking up for the night, the bolt on the main door squeaking as it slid into its cuff. The silence tightened around us.

I looked across at Brucker. One of his gloves was ripped; probably on the fat Cheshire wife who refused to remove her jewellery. The glinting steel of his finger poked through. Garfield would notice this tomorrow. He would sigh, shake his greying head, and fit a new glove. He was good, Garfield. He never missed a thing.

The gentle waves of the diagnostic sequence lapped through my circuits, easing me into another long night. Soon the last touches of anxiety had left and I hadn't even noticed them go. But the peace wouldn't last. Brucker had opened up his soul to me again last night and I had a sense that his vague, intangible fears were warping into some darker terror. He kept asking me why he felt so hollow. I gave him the usual, *because you haven't been listening to your Porta-Pod,* but he turned on me viciously. I wasn't to patronise him with corporate wank. He'd had a new feeling, one where he wanted to squeeze and squeeze and never stop.

Something surged. Messages spiralled into dizzying fractal shapes and the mainframe kicked me up to Cognitive where the practical answers lay. Cognitive Therapy. How dull it was and how I envied Stoker who had an old Freud programme which users often asked for, mainly for fun, I suspected. I loved to hear his carry-on-camping dream analyses in which everything shimmered with sex and envy and death, and the only possible remedies for neurosis were time travel or never having been born.

Brucker asked me again why he felt so hollow and I suggested that he think of something good each time the feeling comes. Of Garfield, with his special screwdrivers and the way they lie in their velvet nests. But he'd tried thinking of Garfield. He'd even thought about how the screwdrivers had specially designed heads to fit his screws and his screws only. But Garfield was the problem. Brucker was having thoughts about Garfield's throat; squeezing and squeezing and everything going dark.

'Your hands are for massage only,' I said. 'The programme won't allow anything else. Spend more time listening to your Portapod.'

But according to Brucker, the Portapods they have now are government-infected bullshit.

The usual methods didn't work. My circuits rippled. Garfield was in peril. If anything happened to him, who would tend to us? I remembered that temporary replacement, a cocky little sod who told us about a new centre in Canada where machines could move about and Garfield's job was carried out by another robot. One of their massage machines had killed a cleaner and they were phasing the model out—it had been in all the papers. His world view seemed to accommodate a hunch that killing people might be quite a deal of fun. He made me feel dumpy and misshapen, alone. Sometimes I wished I knew nothing, that I kneaded flesh and bones like Brucker, or emitted pleasant scents like the ones in the Relax Shed. So clarifying to be unwise, un-desiring.

Brucker sighed and my programme shifted up a step, to drug prescription. But that part was useless for machines. I needed to captivate him with mystery, enchant him with religion, tantalise him with the idea of a god. But I couldn't. There was no magic, they'd forgotten to put it into the codes.

Scruuurk, scruurrk. Garfield dragged his plastic bucket down the corridor towards us. My wires sang with the loss. I knew I couldn't save him.

IN THE DAYS BEFORE
TRICKERY

THE SAX RIFF kicked in and Stan dropped his bin bag. He stared at the speaker. 'That's me.' His eyes were all watery. 'Nineteen fifty-nine.'

Stan's sax break, a tilting bebop figure bending sensuously in and out of a stolen surf-guitar lick, was an integral part of 'Eskimo Strut'. The white label was colossal in the clubs, we'd signed a distribution deal, and 'Eskimo Strut' was set to make a skip load of gravy. But this particular sound-collagist-stroke-DJ-stroke-sonic-sculptor hadn't bothered to clear the samples. After all, who remembered them? Faceless sessioneers parping clichéd horn parts or prodding guitars set to space tremolo, before sloping home to claggy bedsits.

'I blew that riff with the Ross McManus Big Band.' Stan went on. 'First sax. I'll never forget 'cos I had a new reed and it was squeaking. You can hear it.'

I sharpened my focus on the blaring horn, but it didn't sound any different to the other brass riffs I nicked. And I'd nicked a lot.

'Show me the cover.'

A chiffon-clad lovely with long thick eyelashes stared back at him. She was holding a cherry delicately by the stem and nibbling it. Across her large cleavage were the words *abeatin' and aboppin'—ice cool grooves for the modern hipster.* Stan's lips moved as he read the liner notes.

What could I do? If Stan contacted the record company I'd have to shell out a shit load of lucre. Don't get me wrong, I'd share the wealth if there was any. But I'm no billy-big-biscuits. I've been doing this for years and I'm still eating out of the bin.

'It's out next week.' I said. 'You'll hear yourself on the radio. We should celebrate. Come to the club tonight. You'll be guest of honour.'

≈

The audience went wild and Stan took dozens of bows to much whistling and whooping. He supped Guinness after Guinness after Guinness and could hardly stand when we locked the door and began the after-party.

'Nice one, Stan.' I lit a fat joint and passed it to him. 'Bet there was a load of pills and weed back in your day, eh? The old Big Bands?'

'Pot, speed, the lot,' he said. 'We hoovered it up, just like the pop bands—but it never got in the papers.'

'You tried E?'

He grinned. 'No. But I'd like to.'

I gave him a fistful of Special K. 'Take them all—for the full effect. What time's your wife expecting you?'

'She passed on. It's just me now,'

We played 'Eskimo Strut' a dozen times and Stan sat there nodding his head and smiling at the sound of his sax crawling though the static from fifty years ago. The Special K kicked in, he got a bit agitated, then finally he fell asleep. We took him home to his place and lay him on his sofa. I never saw him again.

I remixed 'Eskimo Strut'. The art of a good collage is to make it your own, to juxtapose sounds so unusual, so

66

startling, that the musicians on the original records would never recognise themselves. The new mix was incredible. I was glad that Stan had helped me out. Those old musicians, they really knew how to play, but it was just a job to some of them, like an assembly line, knocking out any old song while thinking about your laundry. Old Stan was different. He had a light in his eyes that danced when the music played.

THE NINETEEN SEVENTY-SIX TROUSER FAMINE

THEY SAY THAT when you die all the trousers you've ever owned flash past. In Derek's case this happened every day. His collection took up several rooms and, at forty-three years old, and still an active trouser buyer, it was ever growing.

Tonight Derek was meeting Hilary. He noted from her web entry that she was a big fan of The Damned, found out when their first single was released, and went straight into his seventies room. But where was the 1976 rack? It was nowhere to be seen. He'd been fifteen in 1976 and, if anything, had increased his trouser-buying in an attempt, along with the care and nurture of his fluffy Zappa moustache, to attract girls.

He rummaged through the other racks. Maybe he had combined it with another year? But there was no sign. He wondered whether his mother had been moving things about, and shuddered, remembering the time she de-alphabetized his packet soups.

This gap in the collection was a devastating blow, and not only to his meeting with Hilary. The integrity of his whole curatorial policy would be undermined if he didn't find 1976. Nineteen seventy-six was an exceptionally interesting year for trousers. It was on the cusp of glam rock and punk, between baggy flares and drainpipes. And it was one of those years (and you only get this phenomenon once or twice a decade) where there was a transitional trouser—in this case, a cut somewhere between a baggy leg and a slim drainpipe. It had been ingenious and could pass for baggy from the front and drainpipe from the side. Derek had owned two pairs of these, as well as various Northern Soul parallels and several slim-cut Wranglers later in the year when punk was really taking off.

He riffled through 1975, but it was no use; some checked Oxford bags he'd worn with platforms and stripy socks, and some stay-pressed which shimmered when viewed from different angles. And 1977 was no better, with its bondage trousers and tartan straight legs. None of these would do. Hilary would notice immediately—a few weeks either way could give you away in the late seventies, trouser fashion moved at such a relentless pace.

∿

Later that night he found himself humming 'New Rose' while he organised his Apple stickers. The evening had gone well. When he'd stood up to shake her hand, Hilary had looked down at his legs and gasped. She had been amazed at so much attention to detail. In fact, it was an even better effect than if he had managed to find the right trousers. She'd been so overwhelmed with emotion that she couldn't continue with the date.

He smiled, thinking of the old Derek charm winding her in. Debenhams, 1976—the power of the Y-front.

WHO READS THIS STORY
WILL NOT SIN

MY GIRLFRIEND WAS a censor and I developed a fascination with the material she extracted from works of art. It would, I decided, be thrilling, potent, uncanny stuff—a billion times more interesting than the stuff she'd left in. It beckoned to me.

My girlfriend loved her job and I loved her. She was my censor, and I should have respected her wishes. But one day I asked her if she would bring home some of the things she removed so that I could have a look for myself.

She refused, of course. No, no, no. She was very firm. The very reason she removed these ugly words and frightening images was so people like me wouldn't see them. Her job was to suck the poison from the veins of society. I asked her if that was what it said on the napkins in the censors' canteen. She didn't laugh, yet despite her indignation, I persisted. If she loved me, really loved me, she would allow me a glimpse, just a peep, into her private world. Eventually she agreed a compromise. She was not willing to bring home actual strips of celluloid, torn-out pages or fragments of videotape, but she would tell me a little more about the material.

And that is what she did. Every evening she acted out an offending scene she'd cut from a film that day. She dressed up, performed the dialogue in different voices, and used props she found about the house. Later, in bed, she whispered to me some of the unruly words she had scrubbed forever from the pages of books.

And don't worry, she would say before I went to sleep. Of all these filthy thoughts and ideas there is now no trace.

We enjoyed sharing these things. It brought us closer together. But was she holding back? Was she describing everything in its full detail? Or was she protecting my innocence?

I became obsessed with seeing these things for myself. After all, wasn't her telling me about them the same? She didn't think so. I was not a censor. She, like the other censors, had grown a protective membrane. It didn't matter what a censor heard, read or saw, they returned to their families untainted by the monstrosities they were forced to endure. But to prove me wrong she would bring home one, just one, of the most horrible things she had ever had to censor.

It was a short film and she was right. It was horrible, so horrible that for days I could not stop replaying the scenes in my head. It existed on some hyper-real plane, in three dimensions. I could taste it, smell it. It pulsed. It was more real than reality itself and I turned it over and over in my mind so much that eventually I imagined I was part of it. I became the perpetrator in the film, and I visited a shopping centre in St Helens and acted out exactly what I had seen.

Some of the people in the shopping centre screamed, many ran away. Some bawled obscenities at me, some shielded their children's eyes or turned their loved ones away from the scene. But the sound I loved most was the gritty whirr of the security camera as it turned on its axis to face me. I looked straight into the lens and hoped that one day my girlfriend would watch this scene and, frowning in that pretty way she had which made a little triangle appear above her nose, take a pair of scissors and excise me entirely from the history of the world.

WHAT WOULD BILL HICKS DO?

ROB SURVEYED HIS seating options. He needed to be near a girl. And not just one girl, he needed two. Casanova's greatest advice: always chat up two women. Two girls compete for attention and in the end agree to anything, to outdo the other. A brace of cute little babes, that's what he needed. He concentrated. He had extra-sensory perception when it came to women. If a room was quiet he could hear the sound of a woman ovulating, a tiny ticking noise like a spider tapping its foot. There they were—two girls, about the same age, and both seats opposite them spare. Their table was littered with magazines, empty coke bottles, chocolate wrappers. These girls enjoyed pleasure, relished the instant gratification of sweet, cloying foods. They lived for the moment.

He waltzed across, gave them the famous Rob grin, the one where he made it lopsided, then removed his coat—slowly, very slowly. A woman watches how you handle the things you own, because she believes that is the way you will touch her body. So he folded it gently, stroked it languorously with his palm, before placing it delicately on the rack above.

He sat down and took out his book—*Men are the Words and Women are the Music*—and pretended to read, smiling and nodding, knowing they were watching. One of them he really liked. She had a rope of hair at the front that had been dyed the colour of trampled candy floss, screaming out against the rest of her closely-cropped blonde locks. He liked her eyes too, the pupils permanently half hidden under her lids, as if her eyeballs had stopped between floors.

He looked into the pages of his book. With a pencil he underlined a section, then gazed off into space. He could feel them watching. Plenty of time. He stretched out a bit, put one leg up on the empty seat, and allowed their eyes to rove all over his long body. He could feel the prickling of their hormones, the crackle of electricity across the table. He would give them thirty minutes.

Twenty-seven minutes later the pink-haired girl asked him a question about the book, and they got talking, mainly about the book and whether any of it was true. They laughed together, the three of them, giddy from the confinement of the train. At this point, if there had been just one girl, he would reach across the table and touch her hand with his finger, brush it lightly. But he didn't do that with two. You had to allow them to decide.

After a time he pulled out the VIP pass. The VIP pass always worked. It gave them something concrete to negotiate over, something that wasn't actually him. It became a cipher. He told them about his stand-up show that night. Would they like a VIP pass? Snag was there was only one. Now he had become their prize and nothing would deprive either of them from winning.

As was usual at this point, the girls went to the toilets. When Rob was working a twosome they always disappeared to negotiate. He once overheard two girls arguing over him, and they argued hard, went through everything each of them had. One was already engaged, so why should she have him? The other had a good job and was about to go on holiday, where she'd meet loads of blokes. On and on like this. He had felt like a piece of meat, if he were honest.

When the girls returned they looked serious. The one he liked looked as though she'd been combing and waxing her pink fly-swatter to impress him even more. She didn't need to.

'So, who's it going to be?' he said.

Pink Hair pouted at him, her cheeks deeply hollowed. 'We haven't been able to decide. Would you mind if we played a little game? Of cards? The winner gets the VIP pass?'

He agreed and Pink Hair produced a well-used deck

'Best of five?' She slapped the cards on to the table and they began to play Three Card Brag. They played rapidly, over and over, as if this was something they did often. They sat extremely close together, like curious biform creatures, each whispering the value of her hand quietly in an odd, wheedling, insect voice. Yet every time one of them was in danger of winning, they raised the number of games. By best of thirty-five, Rob was bored. He gazed out of the window. Next to a field a man was holding a little girl up high so she could feed clumps of grass to a horse. He imagined the man was himself in the future and that the mother of the child was the pink-haired girl. He fantasised that the view from the train windows was the future and strained to see if he could see any other versions of himself out there. There was a man fishing by a canal—Rob imagined it was him after he had gained and lost a fortune in the comedy business; he was now destitute, his only sustenance tiny chub from the grimy urban waterway to be fried at home in stale breadcrumbs from a bakery skip. Here was an old man walking three dogs—Rob after he'd set up a dog breeding business and moved south. How many futures were there out there for him, parallel lives running alongside the railway tracks?

The girls had stopped playing their card game and were sitting still, each holding a corner of the VIP pass. It had been a tie. They couldn't decide. Suddenly the train stopped, the engine powering down with a long dying sob. The carriage was next to a tumble-down house with a rambling garden reaching down to the embankment, a jumble of outdoor furniture, garish plastic toys and plant pots, blurring into the scrubby margins of the railway line.

'Let's not go to the gig at all.' said Pink Hair. 'Let's jump off the train, roll down the embankment and live in that house there, all three of us.' With decisive vigour, she blew upwards from the side of her mouth to dislodge her pink string of a fringe. 'We will sit in that messy garden, drink gin and tonics, and wave at trains. We will go to bed early and sleep to the rhythm of the tracks—*chukka da chuk, chukka da chuk, chukka da chuk.*'

Rob tried to imagine the three of them in the dark house at night, long freight trains rumbling by, carriage after carriage after carriage. He could picture the girls, but for some reason couldn't place himself with them. The girls lay alone in the darkness, bereft of everything, with only each other, wrapped in an endless, inky night.

MEAN PICKING

HOWARD STOPPED AGING when he was thirty-five. He'd been this way for a while, yet his condition disturbed him, and he would often sneak up into the loft, get out his wedding pictures and imagine what the pictures would look like if he really was thirty-five. His wedding would have taken place in the eighties. The mile-wide collar of Howard's suit would be slim and punky. His shirt, its penny-round tips lunging out of the picture at urgent angles, would be tidier, neater. Flapping trouser flares would be replaced with drainpipes. His shoulder-length feather cut would shrink to a buzz-clipped back and sides with a gelled spiky top. And Maureen's dress, hippy-gingham, floaty, would be close-fitted, vampish. A steroid-pumped hairstyle would jut out in every direction as if flushed with static. The sexy Mia Farrow bowl cut Howard had loved would be gone. If Howard was really thirty-five years old then his wedding couldn't have looked as it did. But every time he looked at the pictures it was still nineteen seventy-two.

The Condition. People assumed it was like *Groundhog Day*, each twenty-four hour period repeating over and over. But it wasn't like that. It was like this: you stayed the same age and the world got older. Howard was thirty-five, had been for twenty years and, according to a dozen specialists, would remain so for the foreseeable future. The Condition was shared with his wife Maureen, and their unaging kids—Janny, Toby and little Floss. Maureen and Howard's friends stayed the same age too, as did everyone they saw regularly. And when they made a new friend, that person stopped aging also. Everyone stayed the same and watched the world decay. New technologies arrived, prime ministers came and went, buildings were demolished and replaced, new films and new bands were replaced by more new films and more new bands. No one from the community questioned their condition, even those with whom they had no contact, the aging people with their cracked voices and chewed faces. Over the years, if you can call them years, they got used to it. But still, Howard would creep up into the loft to look at the photo albums and reassure himself. Here was proof that time had passed, leaving its mark upon these mortal, human beings.

He heard Maureen coming up the stairs and shut the photo album, preparing a suitable expression for his face. But she had something more important to tell him.

'It's Councillor Leathley,' she said.

Councillor Leathley was the chair of the parish council. Howard came down the ladders and met him in the hall. Leathley was carrying a banjo. He followed Howard's eyes. 'I was presented with this earlier tonight at the council meeting.' He didn't smile 'You know how I love Country and Western.'

'I know. I've heard you play.'

'It was receiving this banjo that got me thinking, I can't play this stuff properly, not really. My heart's not in it, and you know why? Because I can't feel the pain, can't understand what the country singers are singing about. You know why Howard, Maureen? It's because I never get old. I met you and your family and I stopped aging. Like all the others. And now, everything's too perfect. We discussed it at the council meeting. The split between agers and non-agers has damaged us. So we passed a motion. We are happy for you to stay in the community, but we'd like to limit contact. You and your family will develop separately.' He coughed and averted his eyes, which were clouded with tears. 'I mean, who's to say what's natural? I don't know. I just know that I can't feel the blues in my heart unless I can grow old. I don't even cry at films any more.'

Howard pulled a face. He had not chosen to be this way.

'I'm so sorry. Maybe one day they will find a cure.'

Howard and Maureen watched Councillor Leathley's retreating figure going down the path. They sat on the sofa for a time, digesting the news. Maureen went over to the stereo and put on the xylophone album, the one where the musicians play really fast. Later, they watched some patterns on the TV, new patterns, ones they'd never seen before. They liked the colours and the shapes. Maureen fed and bathed little Floss, put her to bed. Howard played football with Toby, told stories to them all upstairs. Then it was supper from paper plates, more TV patterns, rapid glockenspiel music, each evening the same as the last, the next, and the one beyond that.

Councillor Leathley had left his banjo behind and Howard picked it up, plucking at the strings. The fret board was worn in certain places from the frequent fingering of the more common chords; even this insensible length of wood experienced a lifecycle of sorts—to be born, to live, to decay. He tried to form a chord, forcing the steel strings hard against the frets. His fingertips burned with pain, but he pressed harder. It hurt. This was what it was like.

THE LAST NORTHERNER

I COULD HEAR their tin spades scrabbling underground, feeble grunts of exertion drifting up like the muffled cries of birds. Southerners. A few minutes earlier their leader's clay-grimy head had popped up through the lawn and I'd watched him commando-wriggle off into the shadows. How did he think he would get away with it? This was the north, the only north we had. Southerners were not welcome. I squinted into the dense shadows where he had hidden. Normally I would call security, and the guards—swift, efficient, yet never brutal—would eject him. But today felt different.

Scroll back six months to the government scientist confirming my results: test for grim humour—positive; test for friendliness—positive; test for resistance to cold—positive; test for bluntness—positive. Everything was confirmed; how did it feel to be the Last Northerner? I, and my family, would be protected, of course. The Last Northerners must not be tainted by whispery southern genes. One thing puzzled him though: he thought we would be gruffer. But not to worry. He explained how we would live. We would have our own encampment, do northern things, and speak in a northern down-to-earth way, such as is not heard anymore. Were we, by any chance, related to a lady named Cilla Black? Never mind, that was another line of enquiry. Everything would be good for us at the encampment. We could smoke if we wanted, eat pies and chocolate bars. Our children would attend a run-down comprehensive on the edge of a dilapidated estate. Yes, he knew there weren't any, but they would create one. Especially for us. Those skills had not been lost. We would be caged, of course, but for our own protection. And not all of the time. Had we been to a safari park? Did we remember how happy the beasts had been? That's how it would be for us. True, people would come to stare, but not all the time, and not rabble. Select groups of international scientists. We wouldn't have to dance or perform—well not unless we wanted to. Maybe the odd George Formby or Gracie Fields number, or possibly a clog dance? But we could discuss it, it wasn't strictly necessary. Well, well. The Last Northerners. How did it feel? Where had we been hiding? He leapt up and hugged us both in turn, very hard.

Most days I visited the model coal mine, emerging to be met by my wife in a pinny, singing a Geordie ballad. Then home to the whippets and the iron bath. But today was not one of those days. Something felt wrong. The queasy claustrophobia of the encampment was getting me down.

I screwed up my eyes, tried to see into the shadows where the southerner was sitting. I heard again his friends beneath me, their picks and spoons chewing out a greasy burrow. How powerfully they must yearn for the North, for sooty grid-built towns, for the cosy fecund stink of squalor, for canal-chilled wastelands where teenagers get pregnant by walking arm-in-arm to the sound of a harmonica.

I didn't call security. Leave the southerners to it. Let them dig their tunnels. Let them come. Let more follow, and more, then more still. I would let them in, all of them. I had jobs for them.

PART THREE

LONG PLAYERS

THIS IS ABOUT DIXIE

GEORGE HATED THEM. They stuck their dirty pig noses into his bin. They sprayed stinky juice over his drying socks. They screeched big time. Hair fell off them. They were *local* cats—stringy, drawling, gum-chewing felines who poured through Dixie's cat flap all day and all night without end.

Local. George pronounced the word like he was holding it in tweezers. Local meant something different to George. Local didn't mean you lived round here, oh no. After all, George lived round here, and he couldn't be called local. For local, read mentally subnormal uneducated morons who wear clothes with writing on them and enjoy the later works of Stevie Wonder.

Local people. George didn't care for them. He could understand why they existed, and how they had come to be as they were. He even believed they had certain rights. But George occupied a comfy parallel universe and when they or their cats invaded he wasn't happy.

You don't know how poncey this guy is. Like the time he described the way I was cleaning up the leaves as *interesting.*

I could have booted his smug fat face in there and then.

But this is about Dixie, back to Dixie. Dixie was the Mona Lisa of felines and had to be protected from these alien invaders. The tide couldn't be stemmed by George on guard

83

with his supersoaker for every single one of Christ's minutes, so George bought a Flapatronic, an electronic cat flap which can be operated only by the secretly encoded Flapatronic collar.

The day the Flapatronic was installed I was trimming my hedge, using no doubt what George would describe as an *interesting* technique, and I watched Dixie approach the new cat flap with his usual pimp-roll kiss-my-sweet-ass walk. He pressed his well-bred shoulder to the door and it opened up like butter, snapping shut behind him with a smug and expensive-sounding clunk. Exclusive and personalised for this prince of cats.

There was nothing new in this as far as Dixie was concerned; it was life as usual. But the effect on the *local* cats was fascinating.

A bedraggled ginger tom and a scabby black and white strolled up and pressed their heads against the flap. Nothing happened. The cats looked baffled. But they persevered, battering at the unyielding door for forty-five minutes before giving up and climbing on to the roof of the shed. They spent the rest of the day watching Dixie hopping in and out of the flap with what seemed to be a new nonchalant skip in his step.

What were the local cats thinking? They would be scrutinising Dixie's technique. Was there some sort of a knack to it, some secret method? Maybe it was the way he wriggled his shoulders when he pushed the door? Maybe something else, something more subtle. Whatever it was, if they watched him for long enough, they would learn the secret. They observed his angle of approach, and the way he lowered his head. They weren't quite sure, but was he lifting one leg off the ground just before the moment of contact? Or was he pausing a moment? Did he sniff at the drain before he pushed the door? Maybe that was it. Maybe it was to do with what he ate beforehand, or perhaps it was the angle of his tail on entry. Was it only at certain times of the day that the door opened for him so wantonly?

George came over, dressed in his weekend gear—ripped jeans, an REM T-shirt, Converse All-Stars on his feet.

'How's your fabulous, patented leaf-control system working, buddy?'

Patented leaf-control system. He was so funny, so arch. Here's what I did. I piled the leaves up against the fence until they rotted away. And, uh, that was it.

'The leaf system, as you call it, is working well, I'd say.'

'You know,' he said, 'piling them up against that fence might make the wood go rotten. Just a thought. We might have to watch that, you and I, because it's a shared boundary and if the fence goes rotten then we'll both end up paying.'

I continued to clip the hedge.

'You know, all those damp leaves packed up against the fence?'

I pointed my shears at him. 'Do you know what that pile of leaves is, George? It's a universe, a small universe. Hedgehogs, beetles, ants, all kinds of creatures live in there. We are part of a web, George, a big web, even you play a part, even,' I nodded at his T shirt, 'REM. You either eat it, fight it, or fuck it, that's the food chain, and in the middle of that pile of leaves they are eating each other, fighting each other, and fucking each other and I'm not going to do anything to spoil their fun.'

George looked at the pile of leaves as if expecting it to shift or tremble with all the churning activity within. Then he laughed. 'That's an, uh, interesting way of looking at it.'

'I don't find it interesting,' I said. 'I find it fucking tedious. But it happens to be true, that's all. Everything that's true isn't fucking interesting.'

George walked off shaking his head.

Boundaries. Typical George. Everything is boundaries, defences, walls. Dividing things up, breaking thing down.

I went inside, made a cup of tea and sat down at the kitchen table. I watched the cats outside in the thickening autumn light. Dixie's cat flap had become the door to Nirvana and the greatest cat minds in the neighbourhood were dedicated to solving the problem.

But nothing worked.

Later Dixie appeared again, and one of the cats went over to greet him. This cat must have been elected by the group and he would be asking Dixie straight: Dixie, how do you do it? And Dixie would be telling them everything he knew. Because even though Dixie was owned by that bastard George, he was a good cat, with a strong sense of community.

'Look,' he would be telling them. 'All you do is walk up and push. Watch me, I don't do anything special.'

They followed his instructions but still it didn't work. Dixie was more baffled than they were. He liked his local friends, was happy when they wandered in and out, poking their sticky paws into whatever fragrant dainties George had left for him.

Dixie slinked inside, no doubt to ponder on his amazing skill. And after a time he came to the obvious conclusion: Dixie was a cat in possession of magical powers.

Later that evening I saw Dixie again. He was sitting on a flowerpot in the middle of a crowd of other cats who leaned towards him as if he were magnetic. In the cat world he must have become a celebrity. How would this affect him? Fame would come, of course, with all the usual trappings: cat drugs, all night parties by the dustbins, and wild three-in-a-hedge romps. There would be relationships with other celebrity cats, like the tabby off the cover of Whiskas Cat Crunchies, a cat I bet every tom in the country would like to get to know better. I hoped that Dixie was level headed enough to deal with what was to come.

For a long while everything was perfectly balanced in our cat community. The local cats accepted that they couldn't use Dixie's cat flap, and Dixie strolled about with his head in the air like a film star.

Then he disappeared. I didn't see him for weeks until the day George persuaded me that I should take a trip to the local dump.

'Hey mate,' he called over the fence. 'Much as I love them,' he waved at the old TV and fridge I'd had sat in the back garden for a couple of months. 'Your, uh, outdoor gallery of conceptual art . . . we were wondering whether you needed a hand getting rid? Only I'm taking a trip to the dump this afternoon, and . . .'

'Oh, thanks for reminding me.' I said. 'I was at the dump myself the other day. I noticed they have a place for old fridges and electrical stuff. I'll go this afternoon.'

'Oh, okay,' George said, doubtfully.

It was down at the dump that I saw Dixie. The poor cat wasn't himself. He looked kind of greasy and had a manic glint in his eye that was vaguely hysterical. It was clear that the euphoria of his new-found fame and glory had lasted a short while only. Doubts had set in. After all, what would happen if his amazing powers disappeared? What if he approached the flap and it didn't click open and he thumped against it like the other non-magic cats? He didn't understand his own powers. And with no insight into how his powers worked or where they came from, how could he protect them?

Like many stars, Dixie's doubts and insecurities had sent him spinning into a spiral of decline. So here he was, at the refuse dump, with a wild gang of feral beasts—angry, dangerous animals who'd never been stroked by a human, watched television or been given a wrapped Christmas present. It was sad to see Dixie like this, fallen so far from grace, and I called out his name, thinking if I could catch him I could take him home.

But if heard me, he didn't let it show.

I picked up a knackered old cooker and a rusted washing machine and loaded them into the car. I didn't really want to litter my garden with this stuff, but if it annoyed George it seemed worthwhile.

I was arranging my new junk in the garden next to the TV and fridge when I heard George ringing the doorbell.

'Very funny,' he said. 'But, you know, it's not just me who ... there's the neighbours at the back, and there's, I don't know. My wife is squeezing my head about it. And it's the leaves as well, and . . .'

'Never mind that. I just saw your Dixie down at the tip.'

'That wouldn't be our Dixie. Dixie likes his comfort too much. But we've put a flyer out for him. Didn't you see the one pinned to the tree? Anyway, listen, there's something else. What do you think about the bowling green issue.' He waved his arm towards the park where a little oblong of grass sat manicured and pristine.

'Crown green bowling? George, I'm surprised. You didn't think that was real did you? Let me explain. It's a bit like Morris dancing. They don't really play the game. It's a re-enactment by the historical society—out-of-work actors paid for by the council.'

'Well,' George said, 'the local kids have started to hang about there—drinking beer, smoking and god knows what.'

God knows what.

'So,' he took out a sheet of paper. Ruled lines and signatures. 'You'll sign our petition, of course?'

I took it from him and was about to scribble *Osama Bin Laden* in one of the spaces when Cakeshop Face loped over

88

with her big farm-girl gait. She was holding a sagging bin liner.

'George, it's Dixie,' she said. 'They found him near the dump.'

We stood and looked at each other for a long time.

I knew what had happened. Dixie was on a slippery slope and unable to fight back. A gang of council estate cats would have introduced him to richer diversions—veterinary prescription drugs maybe. He would have become addicted immediately. He would have put on weight; he would have become obsessed by sex; he would have flirted with mysterious, esoteric cat religions, popular in the south of the city. Eventually, after an all-day bender with some self-obsessed ex-sit-com cat, he would have run into the road and, using the same powers that opened his flap, tried to stop the ten-ton refuse truck that was roaring towards him.

The eighteen-wheeler would have left nothing but a flat wodge of fur and blood.

Cakeshop Face opened the bag and George looked in.

'Oh, God,' he said.

Dixie's little body slid into the wheelie bin. Tears were in George's eyes. Cakeshop Face put her arm around him and they went into the house. They didn't say goodbye.

∾

A few weeks later George bought a new cat, a dandified Siamese with a sleek, wry way of looking at me that I didn't like. George fitted Dixie's Flapatronic collar to it immediately. That night I was lying awake, thinking about how George had described the way I keep my CDs in order of acquisition as *an interesting approach,* when from outside I heard a blood-chilling wail and the rasp of fur and fang against concrete.

The next day a gobbet of offal stained the drive and George was standing near the wheelie bin with his shovel. He looked pained, distracted.

'It's sad,' he said, 'I feel very sad. Two in the same number of weeks.'

'I know,' I said. 'I liked Dixie. He had something. A good sense of himself.'

It sounded like something another man might say.

'Did you realise,' he said, 'that the life of a cat is very complex? We have no idea. They each have a territory and it can be as big as a mile or so. They mark it out with urine and patrol it. That's what they do at night, I think. Imagine, a whole alternative map of the city could be developed based on thousands upon thousands of overlapping cat territories. Just think about that.'

He disappeared into his house, shaking his head.

I decided to tidy up the leaves. George was right. We would both have to pay if the fence rotted. It was a shared boundary and as such required care, respect—love, even. For without boundaries how would we ever know where one thing ended and the other began?

DOES ANYONE CARE FOR YOU ON A REGULAR BASIS?

I WAS TIDYING up the leaflets in the Zing waiting room—all lentil weaving, dance-upuncture and 57 different flavours of yoga—when I saw him sobbing into a copy of *Take A Break*. Turned out he used to make wooden peaches, someone nicked his idea and now his business was on its back with its legs in the air. Wooden peaches. Don't ask me. So, anyway, I started talking to him, helping him see the positive side of things, and the receptionist let us use one of the consulting rooms, and I forgot all about my shit I was just so focussed on helping this poor wooden peaches guy. When we'd finished the guy says to Carl, the Zing manager, 'I want an appointment to see him,' pointing at me, and Carl looks at me and says, 'You're obviously improving, Boris. Maybe you're ready to see clients on your own.' So meet the Zing Centre Counselling Service. Yes, I know, but as they say in Hollywood, nobody knows anything, do they?

Carl is alright. A bit fat, but graceful with it—the sort of man you could easily imagine wearing flip-flops. He suggested I handle bereavements, mild anxiety, stress, and was I able to take on terminal illness? Or traumas, such as the violent deaths of loved ones? I said yes, I'd give it a go. After all, what harm could I do? It was talking, that's all, a chat about how people felt, with the addition of my objective viewpoint as a cold, distant observer. I borrowed as many books from the library on counselling as I could—eight different titles. Even a professional counsellor couldn't have read more than eight volumes of this shite.

My first appointment was a woman whose tortured expression made her look like she was permanently trying to expel a rat's turd from her nostril. She had a tiny, fat dog whose pink tongue slipped in and out with a fluttering sound.

'It was the census questionnaire that set me off,' she said. 'Question number thirty-four: *does anyone care for you on a regular basis?* I stared at this question, wondering what it meant. Sat there for hours. And since then I just can't seem to get on with my life. Can you give me some techniques?'

The fat, pampered dog looked up at her and whined, and she brought out a bag of Maltesers which she inserted into its mouth like feeding a slot.

'If I didn't have little Dale,' she nodded at the flabby ball of fur, 'I'd break down. I know my reaction isn't normal. It was just a stupid question on a form.'

I had no idea what to do or say. I thought about the eight books on counselling, but so far I'd read only the introduction to one of them, so I knew very few things. One was that you should show empathy.

'I have a lot of empathy for your situation,' I said. 'After all, what is normal? Is it normal to, say, watch soap operas, watch the lives of other people unfold before your eyes, people you don't know, people who aren't real?'

'Well, the way you put it, it sounds weird, but I'd say it was normal. Yes.'

'What if you drilled a hole in your neighbour's wall and watched their family all day? Would that be normal?'

She went out in tears and when she'd gone I asked the receptionist if she could book in some less emotional clients for me, and she just said, 'Well, Mr Coen, that's kind of the *point?*'

I went back to my consulting room and waited for the next one. Where are the patients with simple problems? Like, say, a phobia about public transport? I could deal with that. I would use toy buses or dress up as a bus driver.

The next one had an expectant, eager look on her face.

'I feel bad,' she said. 'Really sick some days.'

I leaned forward and clasped my hands together.' *You feel really bad. Really sick. Some days.'*

She wrinkled her brow. 'That's what I said. What do you suggest?'

I was lost. What was going wrong? The books from the library said to repeat things, reflect back. And paraphrase.

'You don't feel very well, and you feel actually physically ill some times.'

She sighed, deep and long. She was young, very small, with a bitter, care-worn face and gnarled, skinny hands that she wrung together all the time. We sat in silence but for the drone and hiccup of the new boiler that the builders were installing. I scanned the room for something that could help. The builders had left massive drills and bits of pipe all over the place. A manual for the new boiler sat on the desk and I slid it over. It was open on a page headed *Trouble Shooting.* Down the left-hand column was a set of problems, down the middle a diagnosis, and in the final column a resolution. If only there was a similar table to solve life's problems.

'Lets go back a little,' I said to her. 'How did you feel this morning?'

'Down.'

'But some days you're up?'

'Yes.'

I had one eye on the first line of the trouble shooter column. 'So it's about . . . balancing?'

Her face loosened. 'Yes, I guess.'

'The system—that's how you live—needs balancing. Some areas are, uh, heating up more than others, and not

93

allowing the, uh, energy to reach the other parts. It's about . . . warmth. The warmth needs to travel through one thing to get to another. Do you see? Eventually the warmth comes back to where it started.'

'Yes. I see. But it's also the stress. The stress of just, like, *living*.'

'Pressure?'

'Yes.'

'Is it a closed system,' I said, 'or an open system?'

'Mmm, I don't know,' she said. 'I think quite open, yes, I'm, we're quite open, me and my husband.'

I leaned back in my chair and spoke towards the ceiling. 'It's about keys. Keys open certain areas and close off others.' I looked up: 'Keys, you see. You need to open things up. With a key.'

'What is the key?'

'You have the key. It comes with the system.

'Oh I see,' she said, nodding.

'You see, sometimes a system needs completely draining. Years and years of the same stuff circulating round and round causes, like, a build up, really, of . . . thick sludge . . . all at the bottom.'

'I know exactly what you're saying.'

'Sometimes you have to take everything apart, empty it, and fill it up again.'

'Thank you, Doctor.'

'I'm not a doctor. But don't worry. I know what you mean.'

The clock ticked. Tears collected in her eyes. I knotted my fingers together in the shape for prayer. Tomorrow I would collect all the instruction manuals from around my house. It was just as I had always suspected. Every piece of printed material ever produced contained a personal message for me.

SPECIAL PUDDING

KATHY LOVED CELLAR bars. Something about descending, something about being beneath. Cellar bars were an annexe to real life, sanctuary. Anything could happen in a cellar bar, and in Corbieres on Half Moon Street, anything often did. Today the bar held an additional thrill; Kathy was waiting for Harry Lawson. What does a headhunter look like? She lit a cigarette and marvelled at her new situation. Blew out a rod of smoke, long and slow, enjoying the feel. Christian had hated her smoking, hated her having fun. Well, now she was rediscovering her old tastes, her suppressed appetites. She'd sprung open a giant over-stuffed toy cupboard, stretched out her arms and let the wild, berserk fun of life pour all over her.

The night Christian left her for The Cheese Straw—Fiona Crush, digital artist, 'space' consultant, and senior designer at Jelly Kiss—Kathy had sat alone in the garden for three and a half hours, staring at the house. It was then that she realised since they had taken down the wall between the downstairs rooms you could see right through the house to the park and beyond that, through the windows of another house, all the way to the shops. A young man was walking along, swinging a loaf of bread. Seeing this young man, so far away, was exhilarating; Kathy's mind had been knocked through to another room.

She always suspected that The Cheese Straw was romantically interested in Christian, but had come to the conclusion that the flowers, kissy texts and gushing emails were part of being in the arty crowd. The Cheese Straw was Kathy's boss, so there were lots of parties to attend together and lots of opportunities for her and Christian to chat whilst Kathy spun around the room manically networking, doing all of Jelly Kiss's work, as usual.

Because, although The Cheese Straw was *on paper* the director of Jelly Kiss, it was Kathy who snapped-shut every deal. This is what she would tell Mr Harry Lawson, headhunter, when he arrived. She would tell him all about it. The injustice. The unfairness.

The Cheese Straw had been at lunch when Harry Lawson telephoned, asking for Ms Crush.

'This is she,' Kathy said without hesitation, and when Harry told her he was acting for a rival company who had heard of her work and would she send some stuff over right away, Kathy still didn't come clean. She surprised herself with her duplicity, her deceitfulness. But after all, it was only three weeks after The Cheese Straw had stolen her husband. And Kathy deserved some professional attention. Her portfolio was much more impressive then The Cheese Straw's. 'Your work,' The Cheese Straw used to say to Kathy, 'is a little, well, lo-fi, darling. And lo-fi is so red specs now.' But Kathy emailed her lo-fi designs to Harry Lawson and he got back to her in twenty minutes. The company would love, absolutely love, to meet her. Harry would bring along a contract and they could sign her up right away.

She lit another cigarette and watched the door. At what point would she tell him the truth? That she wasn't Fiona Crush, space consultant, but Kathy Duffy, assistant designer?

She was busy being chatted up by the sexy young waiter when Harry Lawson appeared and had almost forgotten why she was there.

'Harry,' he said.

She looked up at him. A soft, chubby face, features almost buried in folds of flab. Good looking, in a Robbie Coltrane kind of way. Kathy didn't mind someone who carried a little weight. She herself was a bit heavy for her height. You wouldn't call her fat, in fact most men said that they liked her as she was—*don't be going on any diets*. But nevertheless, she tried to avoid getting any larger, especially now that she was 'out there'.

Harry glanced at her plate on which was sitting a third of her sandwich. 'You've left a lot. You on the "two-thirds"?'

It was true, she'd been trying out a new diet. Eat two-thirds of every portion and lose a third of your weight. 'Yeh.'

'It's such a waste. I've tried it and, as you can see, it doesn't work.' He seemed uneasy for a headhunter, not as sure of himself as Kathy would have expected. She began to grow concerned, but stopped herself abruptly. Don't worry. He's fat. Fat people can be trusted. Fat people know what it's like to be abused, ignored; they treat everyone with respect.

'Do you want to finish it?' she said.

'I've eaten.' He sat down opposite her. 'But before we get down to business, Fiona,' she had forgotten. Tonight she was Fiona, 'can I get you another drink?'

They shared a bottle of wine and the conversation flowed freely, moving on finally to the business of hunting her head. Was her current employer looking after her? Was she happy with her situation at Jelly Kiss? Did she think she was worth more? Did she think Jelly Kiss were getting the most out of an employee with such immense creative potential? Kathy agreed with everything Harry said. And why not? He was handsome, he was funny, and he looked at her all the time. So when he asked her if she would like to share a special pudding with him, she couldn't say no.

'What's a special pudding?'

'Well, this is a funny one. To enjoy your special pudding, your dining partner must lick the spoon first. But she, or he, must not eat any of the pudding. Not even a little bit. Lick the spoon, then watch me eat.'

It was an odd proposition, but she had to impress the headhunter.

A glutinous orange blob in a glass beaker arrived. Kathy licked the spoon then passed it to the headhunter. Harry began to eat, very, very slowly, taking tiny pecks of pudding at a time. There was an odd smile on his face as he slurped.

But that wasn't the strangest thing. Kathy felt a new and uncanny sensation that she'd never experienced before. She could actually taste the pudding as Harry ate it. And the taste sent a tingle from her tongue to her scalp and then from her scalp all the way down to the soles of her feet. She watched him chew and it was as if *she* were chewing. Gooey sugar and starch slid down her throat and into her stomach. Gorgeous.

'*Mmmm,*' she said, not realising the sound she was making was audible. 'That's delicious.'

He squinted at her over the orange dessert and smiled. She knew from his wistful, far-off expression that he was aware Kathy could taste the pudding. He'd been through this experience before. Kathy began to feel frightened. Was this a hypnotic trick? Had she fallen under the influence of some twisted, amateur magician? All of a sudden she felt queasy, and stood up quickly, grabbing her things and making ready to leave.

But he touched her arm and looked her in the eyes. 'Don't worry. It's nothing to do with me. I'm not making it happen. I heard about this pudding and what it does, and wanted to try it out. Honestly. Sit down. Let's talk.'

She sat down and looked at him. She said nothing. He said nothing. Then they both laughed.

'How weird,' they said in unison. 'I wonder how it works?' again, in chorus. They laughed again. His eyes were nice when he laughed, little lines shot out at the side that weren't there before,

'God, you know what?' said Harry. 'I could eat some more.'

'More pudding?'

'Yeh. What do you think?'

Kathy thought about it. She had enjoyed the feeling of the pudding slipping down her throat and, if this was a pleasure she could enjoy without putting on a single ounce, it was some sort of miracle. She leaned across the table. 'Yes. Why not have another? Let's have another.'

Cheesecake came and the same thing happened. Kathy watched him delicately spoon in gobbets of strawberry and crushed digestive and again she tasted it, a taste sensation in ultra-high definition, as if every dimension of its flavour were magnified a hundred times. The coldness on her lips, the crumbling and melting on her tongue, the sweet goo oozing down her throat. Yet her stomach remained as empty as her mouth.

Kathy and Harry worked their way through the whole of the dessert menu, pudding after pudding, and though Kathy tasted them all, she felt not a tiny bit full. And the taste! A thousand bursts of explosion inside her.

Outside the bar they stood together for a few moments. Harry dragged a woolly hat from his pocket and tugged it onto his head. It made his face, which bore a satisfied, far-away expression, into a round ball. He laughed and gave her a big hug.

'I've had a brilliant evening. Thanks for eating with me.'

Up close he smelled sweaty, an odour that, though it would usually repel, was oddly arousing and made her feel feral, uneasy.

'What are you doing the rest of the week, Fiona?'

~

From Spanish to Mexican, from French to Greek, from Chinese to Turkish, Kathy and Harry tried them all. Kathy ordered minuscule starters while Harry had the works. She would sit and watch him eat, tasting it all, every bite of steak, every blob of sauce, every mayonnaise-doused chip, every pie, pastry, pudding, tart and bake, and in each restaurant the diners and bemused waiters watched in awe as Harry worked his way though the menu on Kathy's command, she eying him with what must have looked like an eerie, predatory expression.

They had fun. One night they talked about previous lovers and he asked her to draw a cartoon of each of them on a napkin. He did the same. They laughed together at the platform shoes, the fluffy eighties hair, the tank tops, the curious hats. She took enormous pleasure in her drawing of Christian, with his trendy specs, complicated designer jeans, sleek trainers and flouncy floral shirt.

At no point, though, could she pluck up the courage to tell him that she wasn't Fiona Crush. The time never seemed right. He explained how the company concerned with employing her were busy preparing the contract, and when he told her the numbers involved her heart jumped. Six figures! She began to wonder whether she could actually take this new job and pass herself off as Fiona Crush for a few years, to enjoy the money.

There was another distraction. After a few weeks of eating out with Harry, although she'd eaten hardly anything, she looked, if anything, fatter. One morning she weighed herself and was astonished to find that she'd put on two and a half stones. A bulging belly blotted out her feet. Her skin was blotchy and dry, face puffy, neck flabby. She felt under her biceps and gasped; bingo wings. The truth was clear. As Kathy gained weight, Harry lost it. Pounds and pounds slid off him. Off Harry Lawson and straight on to Kathy Duffy.

Yet regardless of the weight gain, she continued to eat out with Harry, because, well, the way he would reach across and tenderly remove a crumb of cake from her lips, the way he called her 'two-thirds', the way he sang Nick Cave songs softy into her ear as they fell asleep. There was no going back from Harry Lawson.

Kathy began to experience the proxy-eating effect even when they were apart. In the office she'd taste his morning croissant; later, a mid-morning muffin, and at lunchtime, a greasy pizza, followed by cloyingly sweet tiramisu.

Then, on Tuesday the 28th of August at 10:23, she received a text. Harry wanted to cool things down a little. For a short time, that was all. He was sorry. Very sorry. He liked her a lot but didn't think they had the same, well, values. That's how he wrote it in the text. *Well,* followed by a comma, then the word *values.* The contract was off too.

She re-read his text over and over, tried to spot where he had hesitated in his typing, where there were unnecessary spaces or where the words were too close together which might mean he had originally chosen a different expression. But the text message was perfectly constructed. She wrote his words out on a piece of paper so she could view the message as one whole thing. He had ended it with a kiss, one kiss only. Their text communications had developed to include three kisses. This growth in kisses had been important to Kathy; she'd been working on increasing it to four. But even though she had used four kisses once or twice, he had never reciprocated. She looked at the piece of paper again. Well spelt (no l8rs or anything for Harry) and grammatically correct. He always texted that way. But what did he mean, *values*? And why, before it, the word *well*?

She called him. But there was no response. She emailed him, but her message bounced back. She rang the head-hunting firm, but was told that no one of that name worked there.

She went up to her bedroom, turned off the light and sat at the window looking out over the sparkling lights of the city. The handwritten version of his text was on her lap. She cried. Tears fell onto the sheet of paper, smudging his words. She was miserable, hated, alone, and fat. Her euphoria at being single again had been a sham. She longed for Christian to return, to leave The Cheese Straw and come back to her. She wanted to be part of the crowd again. To be arty, to be trendy, to be loved.

She looked across towards the city centre, where Christian and The Cheese Straw now lived. She could almost make out the roof of their house, a trendy old terrace converted into what the council called *artists' live/work spaces.* She wondered what they were doing at that very instant. Their home was so close that if she had some means of propelling an object—a missile launcher, say—she would be able to send them a message. She looked over to the other side of the city where Harry had said he lived. But did he really live there? She'd never been to his house, had only a vague idea that it was north.

She pointed the missile launcher towards the north and flicked an invisible trigger. A gleaming cigar scooted up into the air making a lovely curving trajectory over the city and descending into Whitefield. It zoomed along a road of semis, its little nose twitching as the electronics sniffed Harry out, glided through his kitchen window and landed right in his big fat lap, blowing his balls off.

It was an interesting thought, but, really, she didn't wish Harry any ill.

One aspect of Harry remained with her. Kathy tasted every single item of food and drink he consumed throughout the day. Which meant she continued to grow fatter. And fatter. Becoming grossly fat was bad enough, but tasting Harry's food tortured her in another way, because from the type of food she could guess what he was doing.

One night he was in a restaurant. A date. And later, predictably, Kathy's mouth was crammed with the flavour of waxy, fatty lipstick. They would be standing outside the woman's house, snogging. The woman would be deciding whether to invite him in. And Kathy knew as soon as she did because that's when Harry began to kiss her face, rapidly, urgently, all over, just like he had with her. Kathy tasted everything about this woman—the bitter un-rinsed shampoo flecks in her hair, the salty sweat on her brow, the antiseptic burn of defoliating cream around her mouth, the milky wash of cheap moisturiser on her cheeks, the nip of Harry's teeth on her lobes, the sour dead skin flakes as his tongue slipped into her ear.

There was a pause for a gulp of heavy red wine, then more of the same then; then Kathy knew where he was heading.

Down.

She panicked. She had to distract her taste buds, somehow numb her senses. She went to the drinks cupboard, but found only Buckfast Tonic wine, a concoction Christian had bought for one of his ironic dinner parties—the quaff of choice for Scottish tramps. She took a succession of rapid sips directly from the bottle, then gagged. It was cheap, pungent, like sucking rust, but she had to drown out her senses. When Kathy's mouth began to fill with the next, dreaded taste, she retched and rushed to the bathroom.

~

The next day her mouth stung with toothpaste and soap. She immediately decided to kick her life into gear. She called Fiona and said she would take six months unpaid leave. She couldn't explain, and don't ask. That was what she was going to do. Then that afternoon she went to Woolworths and bought baggy tracksuits and cheap slippers. She would dress for comfort.

103

Over the next few weeks she changed her life. She stopped showering, washing only when she felt it was essential, which wasn't that often. She drank Buckfast straight from the bottle, because what was the point of cleaning a glass every day? She got used to its vile, rusty taste. She cleaned her clothes by throwing them into the bath with her whenever she washed herself. All this seemed logical and she congratulated herself on this eminently practical way of organising her life. She would stay in the house and never see another human being again. There was a glum finality to this decision that satisfied her. She was in control.

She was in the bath sipping Buckfast, a couple of her tracksuits and several pieces of underwear floating about her, when the doorbell rang. She pulled on Christian's old dressing gown and went to see who it was.

The last person she expected was The Cheese Straw.

The Cheese Straw wrinkled her nose at Kathy's stained jogging clothes and the sour-sweet smell of Buckfast.

'I hope everything's okay with you? I am really sorry about what happened.' Fiona Crush, bony face the colour of pearl and buffed with expensive lotions, gave Kathy her point of view. 'That man Harry, I heard about it. He was sent by someone else. There was no company, no headhunters. I'm sure you know all this by now. It was all on account of another man I used to know. And had to stop knowing. Some sick joke, I think.'

'Do you want a drink?' Kathy jiggled the bottle of Buckfast. 'It's tonic. Good for the nerves.'

'No, thank you, I won't. But there's some papers Christian and I need you to sign. We've been waiting a few weeks now. You know it's all over. There's no going back. Everyone has to accept things and move on. It's hard for us all.' Her eyes skimmed the room and fell on the mountain of unopened post. 'I guess you've been busy. It's just a couple of signatures.'

'Listen,' Kathy said, 'I'll sign everything, anything you want. It's just I need to know a bit more about why everything went wrong. I don't blame you, but, as you can see I'm struggling to get over Christian. I was wondering, would you meet me for lunch? We could talk. And if you bring fresh copies of the papers, I will sign them right away.'

The Cheese Straw curled her lip, barely perceptibly, then quickly reassumed her posture. 'Of course. Where would you like to meet?'

∼

At Corbieres, The Cheese Straw licked the spoon just as Kathy asked. Then Kathy tucked into the special pudding. The Cheese Straw shuddered at the weirdness of the experience, but said nothing.

After that, Kathy signed each legal paper with a huge flourish of her pen. Tears of happiness streamed down her chubby cheeks. She must have looked like a fat, red pig. The two women cheek-kissed with a vow to do lunch again—soon, very soon.

Over the next few days Kathy ate like a rat. She pictured The Cheese Straw weighing herself every morning and gasping as the pounds clocked on. Would she have digital scales or mechanical? Kathy preferred the idea of mechanical, enjoying the thought of a slim needle twitching up the scale, rather than the flickering of cold red digits.

Kathy's weight peeled off. She threw out the tracksuits. She began washing again. She stopped drinking Buckfast. She got herself a new boyfriend, Ray, a housing consultant and amateur flamenco guitarist.

∼

She was out shopping with Ray on King Street when she saw them. At first, she thought Christian was pushing a pram, and with horror imagined they'd had a baby. But it wasn't a pram, it was a wheelchair. And sitting in it was The Cheese Straw. A shapeless jogging suit covered legs the thickness of tree trunks and a stomach that looked like she'd ingested a space hopper. Kathy thought about the Caesar salad she'd eaten for lunch and the side portion of potato wedges and felt abruptly queasy. All the food she'd eaten paraded about town as a horrifying blob on wheels.

Kathy pulled Ray into a shop doorway and they waited for the couple to pass. As they did she saw them close up. The Cheese Straw had lost all her facial features, as if her head had been inflated with a pump. Christian's face was creased and emptied of colour. A thought came unbidden into Kathy's head; she wondered if they still made love, and gagged at the idea. She couldn't stand the idea of Christian so unhappy, hated that he was chained forever to this monstrous whale-woman.

She had to do something.

$\sim$

Upstairs she slipped into a purple nightgown. You had to wear purple, everyone knew that. She took out the ingredients, measured out the quantities as the website had directed, and laid it all out in a row of little pyramids. It was as if as she were organising spices for a special meal. She'd had to run all over town to the get the things she needed; chemists, DIY shops, even a builders' yard. She scooped up each hill of powder with a teaspoon and mixed it into a mug of hot chocolate. A sticky sludge formed at the bottom. She drank it down in long, heavy draughts, panting between gulps. Beads of sweat were on her brow. She felt her pulse. It was normal. She felt her head. No temperature.

She went to the window and sat there, looking out. She rang Christian on his mobile. He was surprised, very surprised to hear from her. They were settling down to watch a DVD. She must have heard that Fiona had been ill, not really herself.

'Christian, I'm dying,' she said. 'I need you to come to me. I've taken something. Come now.'

He was silent for a long time. Then she heard him murmuring something to The Cheese Straw. 'Okay, okay.' he said. 'I'll be there.'

She heard him grabbing his car keys, then he hung up his phone.

It was a steamy hot night. Everything was completely still. You could hear noises from all over the city. Lorries changing gear on the motorway as they climbed the slip road, voices leaving the pub down the road. She looked over to where Christian and The Cheese Straw lived. Again she imagined she could see the roof of their house. She waited a few minutes, then took out a cigarette lighter. She snicked the ignition, lifted it to her mouth, and opened wide. She sucked hard. A ball of hot air rolled down into her stomach like a fiery gobstopper.

On the other side of the city, flames swathed the rooftops orange and there was an enormous bang. The glass in the window trembled. A plume of smoke rose up. Car alarms sang—one, then another, then another. The air crackled, eased, died, leaving a temporary silence. A few moments later, sirens wailed. People shouted, screamed. Could she hear sobbing? Was it possible from this far away? Maybe it was the thrumming of blood in her head.

Christian was on his way home. He was safe, and would be all hers again. The Cheese Straw—Fiona Crush, digital artist, 'space' consultant, and senior designer at Jelly Kiss —was gone. Here at the window sat a new woman. She would be his special thing, his special friend, his special love, his special pudding.

GUIDED BY VOICES

Anthony Burgess was having a problem with his computer. The letter he was composing kept disappearing. Gifford knew it was just a *control-N* miss-hit, but he listened calmly as the Burgess man ranted away about the pointless march of technology, the pure alienation, and what was wrong with typewriters? Gifford's microphone, a cute bobble on the end of a gorgeous curving stem curling out from his ear, waited to transmit his advice.

It was five past four in the morning.

'What are you trying to achieve, Mr Burgess?'

'I'm writing a fucking letter; a letter about this gypsy picture for the fucking Burgess gift shop. I am to suggest products. Have you, young man, heard of Billy Bass?'

'They have one in my chip shop. You press a button and it sings *Take Me to the River*.'

'Indeed. Well, the mechanical picture I have devised will have a similar appeal. Where is this chip shop?'

'Prestwich.'

The caller fell silent for a short time. 'And how are your neighbours—my lovely, dirty Harpurhey, my Miles Platting?'

The man sounded very, very old.

'Harpurhey? Miles Platting? They're fine,' Gifford said. 'You don't sound Mancunian, Mr Burgess.'

'I've lost a lot of my background. Tell me, as a fellow Mancunian, is it possible to erase your background completely?'

Gifford looked at the dusty screen behind which slabs of data crouched, poised to shudder into life at his command. He moused through the script and clicked 'background'.

'Where no background is specified it will appear as the default background of the person viewing it.'

Burgess made a spluttery sound. 'What's the default?'

'Grey, usually.'

'One. Long. Grey. Saturday.'

'That would be Morrissey, right?'

'Morrissey, wrong. Anyway, the gift. When I was little I was terrified by a picture of a gypsy woman that hung above my bed. At night the picture spewed out horse faeces and snakes. So, this gift item, you hang it on the wall, press the button and . . .'

'I see.'

'Would you buy one?'

'The only question in my mind,' said Gifford, 'is, would one be enough?'

Talking with this Burgess man was odd, unsettling. Something crouched behind his words, something dark, pulsing.

∽

The next morning Gifford told Debbie about his strange caller and it turned out she'd heard about him, even tried to read his impenetrable books. Gifford had heard only of *A Clockwork Orange*. Alongside *Confessions of a Window Cleaner* it was a cultural totem from his youth. It had beckoned to him, speaking of a sticky, pungent world of sex and blood and power.

Debbie left for work and Gifford sat on the sofa, wrapped in a duvet. He tried to sleep but couldn't. It was impossible to find the beat with these permanent night shifts. He switched on the shopping channel. The presenters brought enormous enthusiasm to every product; he wished he could do the same. He was so bored. Since he left the army he couldn't get used to the responsibility of filling his own time. He looked forward to his shift. The soft burring voices and the juicy clack-clack of the keyboards. Warm sounds, gooey. A big nest. Gifford liked giving advice on computers. Better than the last place, sales, where they tied a helium balloon around your neck each time you failed to close a deal. On his first night, Gifford nearly floated away.

His solicitor rang. He hadn't forgotten about the court case next month, had he? He had. Because there had been only one thing on his mind. The strange Burgess man. Something unsaid had spiced their conversation and it tapped away inside his head like a larvae.

∼

At exactly five past four Burgess called again. 'The whole fucking thing,' the old man roared, 'seems to collapse under its own complexity. I've deleted it. Has it gone for good?'

'No. You can recover it.'

'So, always a trace, always its soul remains.'

'You just need to have confidence, Mr Burgess, faith.'

Burgess was silent for a long time. Gifford could hear him slurping at something, then sniffling.

'Faith.' His voice was increasingly slurred. 'And to test my faith?'

'Try switching it off and then back on again.'

'Switching it off? Doesn't work. The catholic flaw.'

'In computers we don't say flaw. We say design side-effect.'

Burgess laughed, a deep rich chuckle. 'When we are speaking, you and I, young Gifford, we have our very own island; we are a civilisation of two.'

Burgess hung up, and Gifford stole a piece of idle time. He looked around the office, loving it all. His own square of carpet, the secret codes, the work-arounds, the down-time, the late night lazy chats, the secret, huddled-up cosiness with disembodied voices. He liked the dimness of it, the way they kept the lights low for the night shift.

Out the window he could see into a launderette, a few early risers sat in there, as if frozen in a cube of light. One of them, a young woman, looked interesting. He could go out there now and get her into conversation. But he shouldn't. Not until after the hearing. The figures in the launderette looked ill, bruised, alone. Gifford pitied them. For Gifford had a friend. A connective tissue had grown between him and Burgess; he felt bereft each time the old man hung up, as if some part of Gifford had been smashed to pieces.

∽

Skin care hour. Remove the visible appearance of wrinkles within days. Showgirl fingernails holding aloft a tiny tube. Ticker tape phone numbers scrolling beneath. Gifford laughed at their jokes.

His solicitor rang. Had Gifford changed his mind? Gifford hadn't. What was the point of the system if you couldn't plead what you wanted? The solicitor kept droning on about the mother's witness impact statement. Gifford slammed down the phone and picked up his copy of *A Clockwork Orange*. Despicable, from the first sentence. It had a special dictionary, and reminded Gifford of books that came with maps. He hated books that pretended they were real. Who needed to grapple with maps of imaginary worlds when the real world was difficult enough to negotiate?

Worse, there were similarities in the book to Gifford's case. He'd been stung by *A Clockwork Orange* and its barbs were still inside him.

~

That night at five past four, Burgess became emotional. Gifford's advice was really helping. Gifford was his middle C.

'Find middle C and everything else will follow. You and I don't need anyone else. That's why I've spoken with Debbie.'

'With Debbie?'

'Yes. With Debbie. I've told her. You're not right for her, not at all. So I had to have a word with her. I told her all about it. Someone had to. Now she knows. There won't be any more problems. You won't have to skulk around hiding things. Best to be open.'

~

Gifford didn't see or hear from Debbie again. He was confused and spent the next day alone, wandering around the places Burgess used to live. In Harpurhey he stood in a whipping wind next to a row of eager but defeated-looking shops. Cartridge World, The Catholics' Children's Rescue Charity Shop. In Moss Side he stood on Princess Road and watched the cars swish by. The police had cordoned-off an area where a young boy had been shot. Ultra violence. Gangs.

At home the solicitor rang again. There had been a development. The others were changing their story. Had Gifford been thinking along the same lines? Gifford didn't understand. He'd been acquitted. Why had the rest of the gang changed their pleas? No, no, no. Gifford wasn't to refer to them as a gang. Gifford told the shrill young lawyer where he could shove his change of plea. What would Anthony Burgess do? Everything returned to Burgess. His relationship with Burgess had warped into a darker dependency, complicating the idea Gifford had of himself as an independent man, able to choose.

Later, alone, he cried. He missed Debbie and when at five past four Burgess rang, Gifford spilled his soul and told him how desperate he felt.

'A woman's system is a queer thing.' Burgess said. 'Mind and body are intermingled. More so than in a man. Fucking fuck her, that's what I say. Fuck her to fucking fuckland. Anyway, I rang to tell you about my new idea for the gift shop. A musical box that emits the sound of three pianos playing different tunes at once.'

'I'm getting so bored with these calls, Mr Burgess.'

'That's funny, because that's something your landlord said. That you seem bored. He says you watch cheap shit on the telly all day.'

'My landlord? You've been speaking to my landlord?'

'Yes. I told him about it all too. It's probably for the best'

Gifford prodded the end call button, threw his teleset onto the desk, logged out of his turret. He went into the kitchen, got Coke from the machine and gulped it down. He talked to a young man about football. He read a newspaper. He looked out of the window into the launderette and saw the young woman again. She was outside, smoking, holding the cigarette at a vampish angle by the side of her head.

∼

Gifford gathered his things from the flat and took them to work where he stored them in his locker. It wasn't a problem. He would sleep in the office during the day. There was a warm cupboard. It would be fine. He would save on rent, buy a car, pull up next to the woman outside the launderette, offer her a lift. When the case was over, of course.

Later, during his shift, Gifford felt tired. They hadn't let him lie in his duvet and watch the shopping channel. His back was stiff, his neck sore, his head hurt. More than Debbie, he missed Burgess. He wished to live the man, eat the man, consume the brand of his life. So that night at five past four Gifford asked Burgess for advice.

'I'd like to go back. Back to before it happened.'

'You've heard of "restore system settings"?'

'Of course. I told you about it.'

'So, choose a date when something changed, something important, and then ask for everything to be changed back to how it was before that date. You know the date.'

Gifford hung up and right away his supervisor came over. She'd been speaking to a man earlier, a caller, an old man. Was it correct, the things the old man said about Gifford? Gifford assured her that, unfortunately, it was.

~

The next day there was a new air of impermanence about the city, as if it might suddenly cease to exist, or melt. He wandered from Moss Side to the university, tracing the steps Burgess had taken all those years ago. He knew Burgess was there, watching him, following, waiting. What had happened to the famous duo, Gifford and Burgess? Their friendship lay depleted, an ugly stump.

He ended up in the Holy Name Church. The smell of incense and disinfectant. An organ played muted diminished sevenths. He opened a confessional and went inside. He stared at the gauzy grill, its velvety curtain blocking the view. Someone entered the other compartment. He heard an old man moan softly with the effort of sitting down, the ruckle of a curtain pulled.

Burgess. He could see his be-hatted silhouette through the grill, smell tobacco, tinned tuna fish and cheap shaving foam.

The man's voice was fruity, clear, undistorted by electronics. 'I went to old Moss Side. They should have pulled it down. Years ago. It's the refusal to believe in original sin that leads to these horrors. Ikea, cheese in tubes, the music of Elton John. What sins do you have to confess, Gifford?'

Gifford told him. He had never told anyone before. This was the first time. It was good to get it all out. Easier than speaking to the police, the courts, his solicitor. Here was a man who understood. When he finished telling, he cried. Burgess was silent.

'It happened to my wife,' Burgess said finally. 'A long time ago. First wife. Army men too. She never recovered. She drank, drank it all away. Now I have to go. Thanks for the advice on my computer. You gave me the gift of a brand new vocabulary.'

Burgess left the confessional box and Gifford peered out after him. A figure in a gaudy waistcoat and ginger tweed suit stood before a stained glass window, rimmed in dancing dust motes. Gifford called out, but it was too late.

In the apse, Gifford stood looking into the giant clamshell of holy water that stood by the door. He wondered what his supervisor had written about him. The file would live forever, his life in binary code, destined never to decay.

He was desperate for somewhere to sit down, somewhere warm, somewhere with people.

He set off towards the laundrette.

GOSSAMER

JUST TELL HER. Open your heart and spill it out. That's what other people do.

But Damien's plan was special. Everything in the universe was clicking into place and all things rang with Emma; even the muted throb of the car's engine sang her name—*Emma, Emma, Emma*. He looked in his rear mirror at the diminishing oblong that was Industry House. Emma would be sitting there this very minute, next to Damien's empty desk. Every evening she lingered in his thoughts. Did he exist in hers? He was about to find out.

At the junction he hesitated. Usually he turned right and headed straight for junction nine. Fourteen minutes and three junctions later he'd roll off the slip road and another eight minutes thirty saw him in his flat eating toast and staring at the fridge. But tonight was different. Instead of turning right, he turned left, then left again, and into Tesco's car park, where he stopped. He laughed and slapped his hands on the steering wheel in a rapid tattoo. '*Woo-hoo!*' he cried, self-consciously. Exuberance didn't come easily to Damien; he couldn't understand why people whistled and hollered out at concerts—he was unable to find the motivation within himself, even though he was sure he enjoyed the gigs as fully as he was intended to. Tonight was different. A new life was spread out before him, a life that would give the answer the one question that mattered; could Emma love him as he loved her? He sat for a time listening to the ticking of metal as the bonnet cooled down. Then he glanced at himself in the rear mirror.

'Bye-bye, Damien Jones, legal consultant. Nice to know you.'

In the Tesco toilets, Damien's transformation took place. He climbed into baggy blue overalls, glued on a false beard, jammed a woolly hat onto his head and balanced a pair of giant green-tinted spectacles on his nose. He nodded at his reflection in the mirror, made a gun with his finger and pointed. 'Hey! Kev! Kevin. Kevo. Kevvy. Kay. Kev. K.man. The K-Miester. What's going on, mate? What's going on pal, mate, pallo. What's happening dude. Hey, how *you* doing? How's it hanging? What's going down . . . dog. Dog? What's new? Hey, lad, what's the crack? What's new, fellah?'

More of this, and more, and yet more, until slowly, incrementally, Damien, the dull, be-suited legal consultant disappeared and Kevin the down-to-earth cleaner nodded and smiled back from the mirror. There was a bold swagger in his walk when he left the supermarket toilets. Mr De Niro was immersed in his role.

Back at Industry House he waited for the security man to buzz him through. Normally the man would have recognised him and given him the ironic half salute he seemed to reserve for Damien and Damien only. Damien could never think of anything to say to the security men. Some of Damien's colleagues chatted away to them, but Damien had no idea what they spoke about. He didn't even know the names of the security people, never seemed to need to. *Mate* was always enough.

∾

Donny, the shift supervisor, had constructed a miniature living room in the corner of the utensil cupboard—coffee table, stool for his feet, pile of *Daily Mirrors* for cultural diversion and an armchair in which he was sitting, sipping from a jam jar an amber liquid the consistency of varnish. A tiny radio on the front of his baseball hat emitted the soft drizzle of drive-time pop. Damien had no idea there were people in the utensil cupboard. He was entering a new world, all the more fascinating because it was hidden away inside the same building in which he worked during the day.

'Here,' Donny said. 'Have a look at this.'

Damien went over and Donny showed him a Polaroid of a crumpled bundle of blankets with, sticking out of it, a tiny baby's head, red and wrinkled like a monkey's.

'My grandson,' he said. 'Two pounds only, that's what he weighs. Born last week.' He slid the picture back in his wallet. 'He's in an incubator, ventilated at the moment, but they expect him to be breathing for himself in a few days.' Donny's eyes were filling with water.

'I'm sorry. They can work wonders now, you know.'

'I know. His oxygen level is a bit high. The mix, you know? Forty per cent. Normal is twenty-one per cent, so they need to get it down to twenty-one. I didn't know there was twenty-one per cent oxygen in the air, did you? I thought it was all oxygen, to be honest.'

'Your grandson looks great. I'm sure he'll be okay. I'm the new fellah by the way. Kev.'

Donny indicated a sheet of paper blu-tacked to the back of the door. 'Take a look at the rota. You're on bogs.'

'Sorry Donny, I can't do toilets. My, er, skin condition—I did tell them at the interview.' He hadn't gone to all this trouble to be stuck inside the toilets, seeing no one. The whole idea was to hang about near Emma, get her talking and find out what she really thought about him.

Donny twiddled the volume knob on the side of his baseball cap. 'What?'

'The skin condition. Didn't they say?'

Donny pushed his lips out, emitted a long puff of air and twiddled up the volume on his hat.

∽

Plucking fag ends from lukewarm urine puddles and wiping slithery snot trails off the tiles did not help Damien in his quest to discover the secrets of Emma's mind. The only advantage to being on toilets was the faint thrill to be had from cleaning the seats in the women's cubicles and, to be honest, even that wasn't worth it. He was about to pack in the job altogether when Donny asked to see him in the utensil cupboard.

A new lamp sat on the table, its light softened by a coloured cloth Donny had thrown over it, giving the room a gelatinous green glow. There were sofa cushions on the floor which weren't there before, and Donny indicated Damien should sit down on one, which he did. Donny lifted a demijohn out from behind a metal cabinet and poured two servings of his viscous brackish brew into jam jars.

'You'll join me, won't you? Tomato wine. I make it myself. Sometimes I sit here and listen to the music, sip the wine. It's like a little island away from everything.'

'I bet,' Damien said. 'How's your grandson?'

'He's, he's not that good. He's, uh, he's had a stomach infection and they had to scan it. And then one of his lungs collapsed and they had to put a machine on him to drain that. So he's in the wars to be honest, not so good. Tough little mite, though. But I've been doing my garden plan.' He nodded his head towards a pile of graph paper on which were drawn neat circles and oblongs and a winding path. 'For when he comes out. Me and the missus, we're gonna

119

make that garden for him and he'll be round when his mum's at work. His mum's on her own you see, so she'll need us. And in a city, you need a garden. At the moment it's a humungous empty space—all lawn.'

Damien looked at the diagrams and Donny explained which were planters, which were beds, which were raised, everything. He had a sheet of paper on which the cost of all the materials was laid out in a complicated matrix of heading and sub-totals, above a timeline showing completion dates for each element.

'If he's out by next month we will have made a start. From next month's salary I'll get the top soil, from the next I'll get shrubs, the month after that the rocks for the rockery. You see? It'll all be great. When he gets out. No pond by the way. You'll have noticed that. No pond 'cos of little Sid, see?'

'Oh,' said Damien.

They sat in silence for a few minutes.

Then Donny said, 'You can re-tune the radio if you want. It's in my hat. I bet you wondered where the music was coming from.' He chuckled. 'A radio in a hat. My daughter got me this. Sid's mum. It was a joke present, I don't imagine she thought I'd wear it. But I do. Come on, you tune it in. The tuning knob's here,' he tapped the side. Damien said he was happy with the station as it was, but Donny shook his head. 'No, no, no. You're young, put something else on. Whatever you want. You've got ten minutes before your shift starts. Enjoy yourself.'

Damien turned the knob on Donny's hat. The speaker whistled, squealed, spat static, hissed at him, but no other station could be found. Fuzzy voices pulsed in and out below the crackle, but he couldn't catch them, couldn't get the right notch on the dial. Donny's breath smelt of instant coffee, toothpaste, foul tomato wine and he wanted to move away as quickly as he could.

'I can't,' Damien said. 'You'll have to do it.'

'Okay, Okay,' Donny said, 'Sit down. What I've really asked you here for is about your work in the toilets. This is a piece of card onto which I have sellotaped an object. The item was found,' he paused and levelled his face at Damien's, 'on one of your toilet seats.'

Suddenly they were Damien's toilet seats

'What do you think it is?'

'I think it's a hair.'

'It is a hair. And what sort of hair do you think it would be on a toilet seat?'

'Well, Donny, you know, there's bound to be the odd one. Toilets aren't really my thing, I think I'd be better off doing the office. My skin, you see. Remember I told you about my skin?'

Donny took a sip from his jam jar and Damien did too and they both looked at the hair sellotaped to the card.

'What are you doing to do with it?' Damien wondered whether it would be filed as part of his personnel record. But Donny picked it up and flipped it over his shoulder. 'You have my full respect as a professional,' Donny said. 'I didn't find that hair on one of your toilet seats. It's one of mine. It was a test, to see whether you would lie. But you didn't. You admitted that you weren't perfect and agreed that it could have been there, that you could have missed it, and that's good. I like a man who recognises his imperfections. I'll tell you what I'll do for you. From tomorrow night you can do the office. Dawn will go back to toilets. She likes 'em any-way, and she's good at it. Damn good.'

≈

To clean his own office. This was what Damien had been waiting for. The next evening he applied his beard glue and polished his oval Reactalites with a quiver of excitement. For the first time he would be somebody else. He would hear what Emma said about him when he wasn't there.

It was strange to see his desk from a new perspective. It looked dirtier than he'd expected. Why had he left it so untidy? Case files all over, some gaping open, innards disgorged, revealing confidential case information for anyone to read. How was he expected to clean a desk in this state? How thoughtless the daytime Damien was. There was even a half-drunk cup of coffee he hadn't bothered to take into the kitchen. It would be he, the evening Damien, who would make this trip, tip the fermenting contents in to the sink, rinse the cup and place it in the dishwasher. How difficult would it have been for the daytime Damien to have done this? Not very difficult at all. There were scraps of paper on the floor that had missed the bin and here was a chewing gun wrapper that he'd just left sitting on the desk. What a slob. Damien was learning so much about himself already. He looked at the way the daytime Damien had personalised his desk; the postcard from Blackpool he'd thought so ironic looked, from this new vantage point, like a clumsy advertisement for a quirky personality, an attribute that, in honesty, Damien did not possess. And the gig tickets he'd stuck up as proof of an active social life had become more crinkly and faded than he'd realised. Damien moved a few things about and dragged a cloth up and down listening to the conversation Emma was having with Rebecca.

'What do you think of this lipstick? Too bright? My lips are so fat. I think this deep colour over-emphasises them. You know what I've got, Becky? I've got big, plump, near-to-exploding bicycle tyre lips' Emma moved her lips apart making a popping sound. 'Look at me, I'm like a fat ugly fish.'

Emma's lips were indeed special. Like an over-engineered solution to some problem, something sexual, possibly.

'No way,' said Rebecca. 'You've got good lips. Emphasise those *lips* girl. Those lips are your ATTACK BRAND.'

Emma broke into a larky smile. 'You think so, darling?' She pouted into her pocket mirror, Jagger-style.

Damien turned to Emma. 'He's a bit messy, this fellah.'

Emma looked as surprised as if Damien's mop head had begun to recite poetry.

'What?'

'This desk. Messy.'

'Oh, that's Damien's desk. He's mortal busy.' She put away her mirror and tapped her computer keyboard. 'Rebecca, look at this site, here. Haircut One Hundred so *are* the eighties.'

'Should I throw this out?' Damien said, holding up the lump of hematite the daytime Damien had collected from his hometown in West Cumbria and left on his desk as a conversation starter.

'No, no, no!' cried Emma. 'That's one of Damien's *special* things'. She exchanged a small smile with Rebecca. 'Damien likes to collect'

'Sounds a bit of a saddo.'

'He's all right.'

She turned her face back to the screen.

∾

Donny called him into the utensil cupboard the next night, and again he had made some changes. Damien had to struggle through a bead curtain behind the door and a photo of a Dolphin with the words 'run free' underneath was on the wall. Orchestral music whined and parped from his baseball hat.

Little Sid was getting over the chest infection, and he was off the ventilator. He was in oxygen still, but breathing for himself. His oxygen was down to thirty per cent and he was getting back some good bloods. They took bloods every hour to see whether they needed to reduce the oxygen mix. Donny was there last night. Bells clanged, monitors beeped, alarms shrieked, babies stopped breathing, and nurses panicked. One nurse even ran across the ward, pushing visitors out of the way. That wasn't right. It was, he explained, a nightmare. His daughter was going through a lot of stress.

'How's the garden plan?' Damien asked.

'Well, look, I've made a new start. There were too many planters on the last one, and the raised beds might have been dangerous for Sid, so we've changed it around a little. What you think?'

Again Damien looked at the circles, squares, oblongs and winding path.

'It's gravel there instead of grass, and here we'll have wood chippings. See? See? And see this?' He took out a small pot in which a plant the size of a peanut was coiled. 'This is a tree fern. It takes forty years to mature. I can't afford a big one. That's gardening. You plant things you won't live to see the beauty of. In the winter you have to take it indoors and wrap its roots up in a blanket. Imagine that? Like it's a little dog or baby.'

'It's going to be nice,' Damien said. 'Nice for little Sid.'

'For little Sid, yeh. You like this music?'

'Classical? No.'

'Me neither.'

∼

The next night Damien again spent a long time cleaning his own desk, listening to Emma and Rebecca talking about travel. For Emma, every sunset, cathedral, or mountain top was a heartbreaking, moving experience. Damien longed to experience it with her. He watched Emma's mouth as she spoke, remembering his name on her lips the night before.

He's *all right*. That's what she'd said. *All right*. That was good, *all right* was good. He remembered how he and Emma used to chat about some reality TV show. They had laughed together and once, while laughing, Emma placed her hand on Damien's upper arm. One evening Damien had dropped into the conversation that he was off to see The White Stripes and Emma said that she was desperate to see them herself, but Dunc—the bloke she lived with—hated gigs. Before he could stop himself Damien had asked Emma if she'd like to come with him. A thick membrane grew between them. The air tightened. They were both thinking about Emma's hand on Damien's upper arm.

During a lull in the two girls chatter he turned to Emma. 'You know, this fellah, I clean his desk, and I have no idea who he is.'

'Join the club,' said Emma.

'I've heard he's very popular.'

Emma slotted her eyes. 'How long have you been working here?'

'Long enough. Hours and hours scraping shit off this ungrateful bastard's work station.'

'*Jesus*. You need to be less, like, involved with your work?'

'I know. It's just, you clean someone's desk, you feel you really know them.'

'You ever met Damien?'

'No, I'm a creature of the night.'

She stared at him.

'Late shift, you know?'

Emma leaned back in her chair and put her hands behind her head. 'Okay. Describe what you think Damien is like, based on his desk. And we will tell you how well you do.'

Emma's world view accommodated a hunch that all people have a certain level of extra sensory powers, so he wasn't surprised at this exercise. He gripped his chin and stared at the desk for a long time. 'He's single.'

'Ding.' she said. 'But how did you know that?'

'No family pictures, no kids, nothing like that. But I sense there's a special someone in his life.'

'Oh yeh, how do you get that?'

'See all these little postcards he has stuck up? I bet if you took one down it would have a little personal message on it.'

'Well, you're wrong there 'cos I've taken them all off and had a look they're blank, blank, blank. Like his life.'

'Oh Emma, don't,' said Rebecca.

'Well, listen to Houdini here.'

Damien made a mental note to put a few messages on the back of the next postcard he stuck up—something spicy to intrigue these prying women. There was one fact about Damien that no one should ever know; his life had no meaning.

~

The next morning, daytime Damien spotted Donny up a ladder, fiddling with a light fitting. Damien went over, in his smart suit, note pad against his chest and pen dancing between his fingers. 'How's it going, mate?'

'Nothing you need to worry about,' Donny said. 'Soon have it done.'

He wondered why Donny didn't tell the daytime Damien about little Sid and the garden plan. What was the difference? He was a human being, despite the suit.

Later he found a Post-it note on his bucket. *Kev. See me in the utensil cupboard. Donny.*

Donny was in a good mood. He had tuned the station to Radio 1 and a dance track was buzzing out.

'See,' he pointed to the radio. 'For you. Give you a boost before your shift.'

'How's little Sid's chest infection? Improved?'

'Not much change, but last night, I was in there, and we got him out of the incubator and we all had a hold. His little fingers have a strong grip, for someone so tiny. Not feeble. We fed him a couple of inches of milk in a syringe.' He held his thumb and forefinger apart to indicate the portion of milk. 'That's all his little stomach can handle. Have some wine,' he shoved a half full jam jar into Damien's hand.

'You know Donny, I'm not too mad about wine. More of a lager man.'

'No class,' Donny laughed. 'That's your problem. You need to be more inspirational. You know, Kev, I sense you could do better than this. That's why I asked you down here tonight. I saw something in the paper for you and me.' He took out an ad and held it up: *make thousands growing mushrooms.*

'I'm thinking, when the garden's finished for little Sid, I might get a shed and that's where you fit in. You and me, we could be business partners in the mushroom business. They send you spores and you do the growing and then they find you a market. This fellah here, see the quote? He made five hundred a week, just from his shed. From a few spores. What do you say? You and me?'

Damien took a sip of the tomato wine and winced at the rancid taste. 'I don't know, Donny. I haven't got the capital.'

'Where's your entrepreneurial spirit?'

They sat in silence for a time, listening to a rap track followed by some yearning ballad from the latest indie wonder kids, sipping their tomato brew until Donny finally said, 'Well, you know, you're probably right. Mushrooms. You know what they are? They are sinister. Did you know they were fleshy? I never eat them myself. Fungus, aren't they? But others shovel them down. Who's to stop them?'

～

127

Emma was rummaging through some papers on Damien's desk when he approached

'Here he comes, international man of mystery. You know, cleaner man, I can never find anything on Damien's desk.'

'Well,' I said. 'He's a sensitive sort.'

'How do you work that out?'

'The way he orders the items on his desk. It looks like a chaotic mess, but it's kind of intuitive. Means he's good with other people's feelings.'

'Not too sensitive, I wouldn't have thought,' said Emma

'I don't know,' Rebecca offered. 'Damien told me he cried his heart out at *Toy Story*.'

'Male sentimentality,' Emma snorted. 'That's not sensitivity. Sensitivity is what you anticipate, what you infer, what you deduce. It's about putting out antennae. My boyfriend, Dunc, is dead sensitive. Let me tell you what he did last week. I went to the town hall for a council tax form and I had to walk past a long line of taxi drivers queuing up to renew their licenses. I'd forgotten it was that time of year. And seeing them all queuing up reminded me of my dad, who died last August. He was a cabbie, and when I was an eleven year-old girl he used to take me with him to renew his licence, and we'd queue up together with all the other drivers and have a laugh. It all flooded back, and I got quite upset, so I rang in sick and went straight home. And you know what? There was Dunc waiting for me, a big mug of hot chocolate in one hand and tissues in the other. He'd taken the day off. He knew I'd have to walk past the taxi drivers, knew that I'd be upset, knew that I would ring in sick, knew I'd need some company.'

Rebecca looked at Emma for a long time. Then she said, 'Hardcore. I would keep hold of him, mate.'

Damien cleared all the papers off the desk and threw every one into the recycling bin. Emma watched him with her eyebrows raised. Then he gave his desk a really good clean—polished it too. He would never clean it again. Whilst he scrubbed he thought about Dunc, Dunc with his heightened sense of other people's feelings.

~

When he went to hand in his notice he found that the utensil cupboard had changed completely. The bead curtain had gone, as had the picture. Only the chair remained and Donny was sitting on it in silence. His radio hat was on the floor, next to a heap of torn up graph paper.

'Sid.' He coughed. 'You know.'

'Oh.'

Damien picked up the graph paper and began to smooth it out. 'Donny, you shouldn't give up on the garden plan. Because you know what? Your daughter, she'll meet someone else. There'll be another kid, and they'll need a garden the same way Sid did. This garden should be like in memory of little Sid. Little Sid's garden.' Damien touched Donny's shoulder. Donny squeezed his fingers into his eyes. His body vibrated and from his throat came a noise like soft humming.

'You should go home, Donny. I came to tell you that I'm leaving. I'm not cut out for this sort of work. I'm sorry. Dawn will do my shift.'

~

A few months later Donny's wife opened the door to find Damien standing there. In his hand was a gleaming new garden spade, its price tag still attached.

'I've come to help Donny,' he said. 'With the garden.'

She brought him inside. Donny hadn't lived there for a long time. Damien asked about Sid and she told him that there was no daughter, never had been, and no little grand-kids. Donny had a few cleaning jobs she said. As well as offices, he cleaned a ward at the children's hospital. He used to get attached to the poor wee mites, get really choked up. He was a good man.

She took Damien out the back. There was no garden, just a dusty cement yard with a little raised pond in the middle. Damien went to the pond and looked in. Just under the surface, he thought he could see Donny's face, beyond reach, and still receding.

Lightning Source UK Ltd.
Milton Keynes UK
06 November 2009
145917UK00001B/9/P